'AY

Lisa Birma[...] at the mind of a war veter[...] with post-traumatic-stress and OCD is both harrowing and rhapsodic in turn. At the center of the book is the depiction of his relationship with his wife—all the light and shadow of daily life, the epic sense of separation, loss, paranoia, and homecoming. Birman's compassionate novel takes us behind closed doors into a world turned upside down but somehow familiar and totally real. *How To Walk Away* belongs in the same company as *Mrs. Dalloway* by Virginia Woolf and Hannah Weiner's *The Fast.*

Lewis Warsh, author of *One Foot Out The Door*

How To Walk Away is about coming home, often the hardest thing. Otis tells the reader: "I know that numbers are dangerous. I know that letters are also numbers. I do what I can to steer around. Given the landscape. The history." Lisa Birman's perfect book explores the secret byways of PTSD, the pandemic of our age. In original and powerful prose, circumnavigating surprises as they appear, it peels the layers of the onion until healing is within sight. This is the magnificent debut novel by a writer I know will give us many. Birman is a gorgeous storyteller with an ear for shaping language and a talent for creating people we learn to suffer with and love.

Margaret Randall, author of *Che On My Mind* and *About Little Charlie Lindbergh*

How to Walk Away by Lisa Birman is an extraordinary book: at once a gripping, intense, grace-filled story, and a profoundly insightful mapping of minds grappling with the diamond-edged particul[...]
I was struck by [...]
with which it w[...]
return to.

Laird H[...]

How To Walk Away offers a stunning cartography that, through its tracing of phantom limbs and other vacancies, leads us to the "room inside the room." All the while, time is kept, a grief clock sounds, through the counting of steps and the relentless inventory of all that is and all that is no longer. Lisa Birman's moving novel is a tremendous contribution to contemporary war literature and deeply reminds us that in the trenches of war's aftermath—at the crossroads of radically opened and closed bodies—we must rethink the terms of "going on." Here is a visionary book that, long after it is finished, continues within the reader, inviting us to walk towards our most difficult questions. It is a place we need to go.

Selah Saterstrom, author of *The Meat and Spirit Plan*

"Maybe I am being incomplete," says the narrator of Lisa Birman's stunningly beautiful first novel, *How To Walk Away*, near the start of a journey that will take us from "celestial intention" to "all the spaces you no longer meet." Geography, orientation and survival—what it means to choose one direction or number rather than another—perform or unfold a psychic space that is both internal and communal. On nearly every page is a remarkable, fluent and searing sentence that transcends narration to seem, also, as if it is a choice being made in the body of the reader of this extraordinary work of fiction. Here are some examples: "When I first got back, I tried making a map of a day. I needed a system." "I could keep moving through. Other times I figured I could go all night without getting to what I wanted to say." "And that's how we make it home." I am obsessed with this book. I am obsessed with the genius and joy it took to write this book: qualities that shine through the devastation and trauma that also lie at the heart of this brilliant story that allows itself, on every page, to feel something, and in this way, through the body itself, life itself, rather than fate or chance or "sameness": transcend. "Just to remind me that there's a door and that there's something on the other side," writes Birman. And we step through. "Which changes everything." Transcendence here is closer to sensation, to the mixed texture of being fully in the world, than it is to a future space or sense. "If invisible has a smell, this is it. I lean into it," Birman tells us. Or: "How we cannot know or plan to know. How intersections are something worth hoping for. Maybe that's what other people talk about when they talk about faith." Maybe this is why we read. I am so grateful to have encountered the talent of Lisa Birman, which is grounded in generosity, love and an abiding interest in migration as a core human factor, code or concern. I hope that you will enjoy this book as much as I did, when I read it, without stopping, on three successive, late summer afternoons.

BHANU KAPIL,

The Jack Kerouac School of Disembodied Poetics

How To Walk Away

Lisa Birman

Spuyten Duyvil
New York City

Acknowledgments

Sections of this work previously appeared in *Revolver, Milk: A Poetry Journal*, and on the CD *Harry's House*. Thank you to the editors for sharing the work in its early stages, and for making a space for writing.

I am always grateful to be part of a community of writers. Special thanks to Max Regan, Junior Burke, Julie Kazimer, Ginny Jordan, Kerry Reilly, Claudia Wyrick, Claudia Savage, Nicole Siegel, and Margaret Randall. I continue to learn so much from you and your work. Thank you for cheering me and Otis on our way.

I know I shouldn't boast, but I won the family lottery. They are an unending source of support and encouragement, and I am thankful every day (even when I forget to say so). Special thanks to Paul and Nikki for your feedback.

A residency at the Ucross Foundation in fall 2011 gave me the time and space to see this novel as a whole. It was the most intensive writing I've ever undertaken, and only possible because of the exquisite care and attention offered by their staff. Thank you.

The work of V.S. Ramachandran both inspired and kept me company throughout the writing of this book.

ISBN 978-1-941550-02-1
Cover art: Untitled fresco by George Schneeman, used by permission of Katie Schneeman

Library of Congress Cataloging-in-Publication Data

Birman, Lisa, 1971-
How to walk away / Lisa Birman.
pages cm
ISBN 978-1-941550-02-1
1. Afghan War, 2001---Veterans--Fiction. 2. Post-traumatic stress disorder--United States--Fiction. 3. Domestic fiction. I. Title.
PS3602.I74655H69 2014
813'.6--dc23
2014014493

for Nana

C100289T

I can't really sleep anymore. It's too noisy and too quiet. I'm used to the sound of you. I wish I had a tape of your voice. I wish I had a tape of you singing to me. I wonder what you'd sing.

1.

The picture breaks and sometimes freezes:

Memory moves like wind. Sometimes discernible. Following a pattern. A sudden gust. This is where we were. Moving slightly west. An event occurs. The compass spills. And even when we steady. Right ourselves in some private or public way. There's a gap we cannot cover. Unaccountable time.

Most people call it a tree but she calls them family maps. She asks her clients about scale. Some people want the world. Others want a hemisphere. There are always surprises. A secret aunt. A questionable history. A disease that does not fall within the lines.

They give her everything they know and she tells them what's true. The dates and geographies. The marriages. The deaths. How the names change with borders and tongues. How the generations repeat. She shows them the corridors they couldn't find. Asks before she walks all the way down.

I've never been good at stopping. I get on a path and have to keep going. Straight ahead or unexpected turns. I end up where I end up. That she can find a corridor and stop to ask a question. That she can turn around if the answer is no. She's the least stubborn person I've ever met. That's not true. She has her ways.

For our eighth anniversary she made me a map. She asked me first. If it would be okay. It was and so she went ahead. All of my family up to me. She started while I was at Fort Jackson and worked on it for months. She'd ask me questions in her letters and on the phone. I told her what I knew. She interviewed my parents and they told her everything they could remember. Even the things they didn't know were true. And out of it all came this map. All the hemispheres pointing to me. Like I'm some kind of star. Some kind of celestial intention.

She wanted to send it to me but I asked her not to. I was already in Afghanistan and I didn't know how to keep it safe without her. She was my map and I asked her to keep it with her until I got home. It wasn't what she intended but I think she liked it. She sent me a photocopy with one of her letters and I touched each name to make it real. I counted all the people, seventy-two, and all the names, one hundred and seventy-seven. I counted all the lines and added all the dates. The last date was our wedding. 2000. Right next to the line that joined her name to mine.

I told her that for our next anniversary we should make another map. Fill out her hemispheres. It was strange to have everything leading up to me and just her name attached like she didn't have a history. I could hear the static at the other end of the line. We didn't talk about it again.

2.

We rebuild our habits one by one:

I'm surprised to find her not in bed. It must be early still. The light is slightly orange through the curtains. In my memory she sleeps later than me. Maybe I only remember weekends. Maybe I am being incomplete.

I hear her in her office and walk through to the kitchen. I reach into the drawer that used to house the spoons. Pens and scissors. Pads of paper. I check the next drawer. Pot holders and dishcloths. It doesn't seem sensible. This difficulty of finding a spoon in a kitchen.

I'm trying to be quiet but she must hear the drawers opening and closing. I hear her humming down the hall. A tune I almost recognize.

Her arms wrap around me. Her mouth finds my neck.

"What are you looking for, honey?" just as I place my hand on the spoon. I pull it out to show her.

"I'm going to make us coffee," I announce.

"I'm going to make us toast," she says.

I turn around and into her. Breathe her in. Breathe us in. Her head fits so exactly where it always has.

"Or we could stay here," I say. And she laughs. Kisses me.

Parts of us keep connecting. Her hand on my arm as I reach for the milk. My feet in her lap as she butters the toast.

"I like that we have our mornings," she says. "It was strange to start a day without you. It never really got less strange."

This is everything I wanted to come home to. Even with so much out of place. Even with her out of bed so early. This is normal. This can work.

"Are you going for a walk?" she asks.

Like that's normal too. Like that's part of the routine.

"Yeah," I look down at the coffee. "Yeah, I'll go now."

And we separate into our days. Cat down the corridor. Me out the door.

3.

They tell you the return will not be as kind as the leaving:

Which comes as a shock at the time. Usually in the midst of leaving. Imagining ourselves in the worst of it. Because it is not possible in that exact moment to think of dipping lower. Because we know the possible ending and cannot think ourselves there.

And so to hear that a safe return still falters, it doesn't seem real. *Maybe that's how it is for other people*, you think. *Probably they already had problems. But that's not us*, you tell yourself. *We were good and are good and will be better after this*. And then the thought lingers. Wakes you up or stops you sleeping. It circles you. Makes every future conversation, every future touch, a question.

They explain that the other will change in your absence. That they have to change in your absence. They have to move forward. Occupy space. They tell you that you will also change. That you may be hurt. That you may hurt someone. That you will have friends who suffer and for whom you suffer. *This has always been true*, you think. *This is true of any marriage*, you tell yourself. Making everything more normal. Just like the neighbors. Just like any other job, any other place.

They remind you that you're in separate rooms now. You try to keep a line between, but the line wears no matter what you do. So when you get back into the same room, you notice all the spaces you no longer meet. That's when it can break. The disappointment of those first moments. Of not living up to the promises of absence and return. But if you can make a new agreement. If you can put aside the details of who you were before and find the new. If you can remember the small things. If you can let yourself limp along. Not try to get it all back at once.

You don't believe it until it happens. But when it happens, there's a shadow. An echo. You're exactly what they said you were. There's something of a disappointment in it. A reassurance too. But first a disappointment. And so you take yourself back to that moment. Try to remember what they told you. You slow down. And hope that she slows with you.

4.

How to get from here to there:

You can make a map out of anything. Hansel and Gretel made theirs out of breadcrumbs. The border was more edible than it should have been. But even if the crumbs had turned to stone they still might have lost their way. Lines shift. A mountain springs up where it wasn't. A river takes just that moment to snake through. When you're heading towards a house made of cake it's hard to remember that stale bread is a commodity. It's an easy mistake to make.

A dictionary can be a map. There was a guy in my platoon who carried one everywhere he went. It couldn't have been more than four by two and it was always somewhere on him. Not in his pack but somewhere on his person. And if he didn't know the answer to something he'd use that dictionary as a map. He'd open up to a page and put his finger on a word and figure it out. Sometimes it took a lot of figuring but he always got there. Always found the connection between where he was and where his finger was. It helped him keep his place.

I had a notion one time that if I could see all the places I went I might understand things better. Imagine that. A map of every place you've ever been. It's not practical. I thought of it too late. I'd been too many places already. I'd never catch up.

When I first got back, I tried making a map of a day. I needed a system. First I thought I'd use some kind of ink on my shoes. But that seemed messier than necessary. I thought about using string but I didn't want to stop myself from getting on a bus if I needed to. I didn't want a system that would change where I went. Just a system to keep track. In the end I did it with words. I took a new notebook and wrote it all up. I started at midnight and went through to the following midnight. Every step around the house. Even if I was just leaning forward in the chair to reach my coffee. If my foot hit the ground I wrote it down.

From the bed to the bathroom and back to the bed. From the bed to the kitchen. All the motions of making breakfast. Back to the bathroom to shower. Back to the bedroom to dress. I tracked myself moving from chair to bookshelf and back to chair in the living room. I walked myself to Cat's office, paused to say hello. She asked me if I'd shoveled the walk yet. I hadn't even noticed the snow. I walked myself back down the corridor and out the front door. Left to the garage for the snow shovel. I noted each imprint of my boots. Another way of counting. It occurred to me that if I stayed outside I could make a record. Momentary but true. But Cat wanted me to clear the walk so I shoveled the snow aside. Counted each step and wrote it in my book. It was still snowing and I could see a shadow of each step as I put the shovel back in the garage. As I walked back along the path and up to the house. I left my boots by the door when I went in to tell Cat it was done. That I was going out for a walk. My feet felt lighter inside. I noted that too.

I know it changed what happened. Less so than paint

on my feet or a big ball of string. But I spent a lot of time writing things down. Maybe some of that time I would have been moving. It's not a perfect map. I don't know that there is a perfect map. There's always a mapmaker. There's always a kick back.

There's a map of the world in the basement. Cat marked all the places she'd gone in red and all the places I'd gone in blue and all the places we'd gone together in purple. Yellow is for what comes next. There are whole countries painted yellow. Papua New Guinea. Portugal. Greece. When I first left she always asked where I was and where I'd been. I'd tell her what I could and she'd mark it up in blue. But it didn't seem accurate anymore. Blue can't stand for everything. It's a big color but it's not big enough for that.

I told her, "Let's stick to red and purple. Let's stick to yellow."

There'll be more blue. It might take a while. But I'll find it.

5.

I could have found a way:

When we were just beginning Cat would ask about the fives. I would tell her stories about being seven years old and hiding under the table. About sneaking red crayons into my pocket. She wanted to know everything. What games we'd played. When it started helping. When I knew. She wanted to know if I was lonely after. If I'd wanted to go back. Even if it meant going backwards.

She asked my parents about it too. How they knew there was a problem. How they knew that they could help. She wanted to know about the therapy sessions with Lanie. If my parents were in the room. If they watched me through a window. And when she asked I remembered a mirror on the wall. My mother looked at me as if she was right now on the other side. Right now undercover.

"Sometimes," she said. "They wanted us to see."

Some couples promise not to lie. Some couples promise to keep their secrets on the table. To prop open the doors. To break the locks. To tell each other everything and always be okay. We never did that. Not just the words. But the ideas. It was always clear that there were things we didn't know. Things we wouldn't tell. The storms, for instance. The closet. I don't know that it's any worse than unobstructed honesty. Maybe everyone works like this. Bits and pieces of their lives. What we want to show. What we want to keep from seeing.

I could have talked about the last time. About the patterns. It might have softened the ground. Broken the entry.

I believed that it was kinder to keep my silence. Which is not the same as believing she wouldn't have to know. I knew from very early on that I would return with fingers tapping out the count. I also knew that I could find my way around. That she could help me. But I didn't want to ask yet. I wanted to be home.

And so when she asked I told her I was doing well. I told her about the other guys. How some of them had nightmares. How some of them got stupid. Took risks they shouldn't take. I couldn't tell her the details. I didn't want anyone crossing out my words. So I didn't tell her about the unreported concussions. I didn't tell her about the amphetamines or the drunk driving. I didn't tell her about the suicides. I told her how much I loved her letters. I didn't tell her about counting words. I didn't ask her why there were only three-hundred and forty words in the last one. Or tell her that the one before was over a thousand and could have easily been two. I wanted things to be normal for as long as they could be normal. I knew it wouldn't last but it was what we had right then and I was trying to keep it.

6.

It helps to have a form:

Each letter was exactly five-hundred words. No matter what was going on. No matter who I was writing to. Five-hundred words. Including my name and their name and if I was really stretching I'd put the date up top too.

People don't notice that sort of stuff but it helps. It gave me a goal. There were times I didn't want to say anything but if I thought about it in numbers I could somehow pile up the words. I could keep moving through. Other times I figured I could go all night without getting to what I wanted to say. But if I knew I was aiming at five-hundred the pressure released.

I never told anyone about it and no one ever asked. It's not like they were sitting at home counting the words and thinking that's just like last time. The words were all different. Only the mathematics stayed the same.

Five-hundred words meant the letters were all the same kind of shape. Maybe you don't notice a shape until it changes. Until it makes itself unusual. Maybe that's what I was going for. Just the regular letter. Same shape as the last.

I counted the words in their letters too. I never found a system but I counted every one. The longer ones made me feel better. No matter what they said. I figured if someone was taking that much time then I must be worth something to them. That's the problem with counting. If you're not regular you can get to judging. That's why you need a number. If it's always the same number it's always the same message. I like that kind of system. It's reliable.

Even if I thought something about their number I never let it show. It wasn't mine. Maybe they had their own system. Something that worked for them. Something I didn't have to know about.

Five-hundred is enough for a general explanation. A description of the daily. There's room for questions and answers to questions. Sometimes there's room for a dream I had or wished I'd had. There was a lot I couldn't say. Location and the like. I never said the word 'preemptive.' I tried not to complain.

I didn't count the words I crossed out. If I made a mistake or changed my mind. I didn't count erasures even if they were right there on the page.

I always recounted the words when I was finished. Just to check. If there were too many I'd have to cross something out and I'd have to mean it. I couldn't cross it out and figure they'd read it anyway. I had to subtract it. I had to believe it wasn't there. If there wasn't enough I'd add a postscript. Or their address. Or the weather. Maybe some words from a song. However many it took.

7.

She said maybe we should go away and maybe we should have:

She listed off the yellow countries. The possible futures. The shared unknown.

"I still want to go to Jamaica," she said. "Or we could go to Chile. Or Brazil."

I just wanted to come home. It's not like me to say no to her.

"We'll go somewhere soon," I promised. "We can plan it together."

"I don't mind planning it. It can be like a present. A welcome home."

"Soon," I promised. "When I'm better."

"What do you mean by better?"

And I could have told her right then. I was already saying it, but not all the way.

"Less tired, I guess."

"Okay," she said. "I just want you home. I just want you home safe."

It used to be a good thing when she said that. It used to make me feel whole. Like even this far apart we were still okay. We were still what we used to be. But then I was sick and she didn't know and the secret was a wall between us. If something else had happened. If I'd been hurt in any of the ways that you're meant to get hurt. A tangible wound. A crush. A break. We used to talk about that. The phone call. She'd tell me about her friends who got the call. How they turned cold. How the news was always slightly vague. How it left them scared. How they tried to tell themselves that this is it. That now it's over. That now they know. I never told anyone I was breaking and I hid it well enough to make it through. She didn't know I was coming home in pieces. It wasn't fair.

I should have met her in the yellow. Maybe it would have been easier to stay invisible. But there was something in me that had to touch the door to know I was home. I kept seeing my right hand. My index finger on the outside door knob. Like I was pointing inside. And I knew I wouldn't be home until I did it. I couldn't tell her that without telling her everything. So I just told her I was tired, which was also true.

And now we're in the countdown of what to say and what to do about it. She's going to let me get there. I can tell by the way she stops herself from watching.

8.

I want to tell her:

That I know I should have said. That it's going to be okay. That hiding is possibly the biggest problem. That it'll only be until it's over. That I have been here before and I know how to get from here to there. That I remember the mechanics. That I only need the quiet to return.

I knew she would be there when the plane landed. Or right outside there. I knew I would have the time between the plane and the terminal. But that was motion. That was steps to count. The plane was for thinking. For stillness. For understanding what comes next or possibly. The noise of the engines was already different from what I was used to. Twenty-seven years of commercial travel. Three years of military. And I'd come to expect the roar. The mutual landscape.

The woman next to me was working on a report. Checking numbers. Marking pages. I was used to photographs and maps. To sleeping and praying. Everyone going to the same destination. Or thereabouts.

In one of the dreams my parents are with her at the airport. And they see it straight away. I don't even get all the way to them. They're standing in the concourse. Cat and Mom and Dad. They see me and throw their hands up. And I wave and I'm still ten feet away and I see my mother take a step back and turn to Cat. I see her mouth make the shape of, *You didn't tell me.* And Cat turns towards her. And it's a dream so even though she isn't facing me and even though I can't hear her, I know she says, *I didn't tell you what?* And then Cat is walking towards me but my mother is still standing back and she's shaking a little bit and she's clutching my father's arm. And he's telling her it's going to be okay. To calm down. That maybe it isn't anything. And I see her decide. I see her pretend to put it away. There's a moment when we look at each other and almost nod. Like we're agreeing to get to it but not now. And then Cat is on me and we're hugging and then I kiss her and wake up.

It makes sense that my mom would see it, even in a dream. There will be more space with Cat. And even when she sees it, there will be a space where she watches from afar. When she knows and I know, and we leave it alone and see what happens.

The woman next to me was reading when I woke up. She had two lemonades and went to the bathroom three times. I told myself I'd try to stay in my seat through the flight. There was a safety demonstration about standing and stretching when we started. It seemed like a better idea to stay put. To keep things fastened. As much as I could.

I watched a movie about time travel. It was really about a couple who can't get it right but end up together anyway. It took a lot of science and some bad luck. But it worked out in the end and that made me feel better. I know we're not that bad. I know we're meant to work out. Just like we were from the first day. I think about the light. How it was just that once but it was everything. I never saw it again but I can see it still. It's what I look for when I look at her. Not to find it but to remember. To know that it was there.

The woman next to me ordered the chicken. It didn't seem right to eat up there. To pretend that things were normal. They asked me twice if there was anything I wanted. I think it's also the uniform. It makes people want to give you things. I tried to stay quiet. There would be enough words when I got there. Even with Cat. Even without saying.

I knew she'd be alone. That we'd find a way to make the public private. It's our way. It's what we do.

I held her for a long time. I kept holding her while we got my bag. While we walked to the car. I told her I wanted to drive home. That's normal. That's part of keeping the space. She asked if I wasn't too tired but she was already digging in her bag for the keys. Handing them over before I answered.

9.

She likes things a certain way and here I am:

Cat said she had to fill the space. It wasn't about having more of anything. Just making it new. Changing the circumstances. It was our space and then it was her space. And this is the part I don't understand. She said she had to move things around to bring me home. That she painted the window frames blue so I would see them. So that things would be different. She said it was about Tom. They had so little left after the fire. Anything that survived became a memorial. Everything had to stay just so. And so this time she had to make things new. She didn't know that I was also changing the space. Mapping it out. Measuring the possibilities. I didn't tell her. It's not her fault.

Now I notice each gap. That the toaster used to be on the other side of the counter. That the couch isn't all the way up against the wall. She used to have a photo of her and her brother on the bookshelf. I ask her about that one.

"I don't know Otis. You were gone three years. Things move around."

And then the next day the photo is there but on the wrong shelf. I move it back to where it's meant to be.

I try not to let her see the counting. I try to let everything be normal again and to let her be happy that I'm home. I want to be the one to say. She's not one for questions but I want to get in before she asks with her eyes. I don't know how I think that's possible. Strangers could catch me doing it. Someone who never saw me a moment in their life could look at me and see I'm stuck. It doesn't make any sense to think she won't. Except to think that maybe she's looking at a reflection. Maybe she's seeing me before I folded back into myself. Strangers see what they see. But maybe she sees what she knows. Maybe I cloud her vision. That's the hope.

I ask her if we should move things around again. Or maybe paint the doors to match the windows. Make the house belong to both of us. She looks at me a long time and then asks, "What don't you like? What do you want to change?"

I don't know the answer so I tell her nothing. That I like it all fine and that it's good to be home. I take five steps to the chair by the window and sit looking out at the street. She stands in the white doorway a minute. Maybe watching me. Maybe imagining me watching the window.

"I'm going to go back to work now," and then her quiet footsteps. The door closing between us.

I divide the space into fives. I make things fit inside my measurements. I practice moving to camouflage the count.

10.

It's easier to talk about and easier to say:

All the misplaced actions. The craving after details and events. It doesn't matter if the light is green or red. It doesn't matter how long the hold is. There are things we cannot tolerate. Services we can't abide. There's a moment when the tone turns over. When you no longer know yourself. It's possible to return from there. But it's easier to continue. To follow the path even when we know it's broken. Even when we know we'll come to harm. It's easier to make believe. To pretend we're in the normal. To keep the motion going. Even when we want to stop. To make amends. To take things back. To start again.

This much time has passed and more is in the balance. All the waiting. The explanations. It's the starting over that does me in. There's always another version of events. It might be easier without a body. Easier to never start. To burrow under covers and desire.

I have never been good with paperwork. The details blur. I lose the thread of what was wanted. Find myself in unfamiliar places. Unremembered agreements.

Every couple finds a balance. What works and when. What joins and what remains in separate spaces. We do not talk about the details but we've always understood them. The papers are Cat's. I'm in charge of carpentry and bookshelves. Scheduling is hers. Gardening is mine. Shopping for groceries is together. Shopping for clothes is separate. All of this fell apart when I was gone. Everything was hers. I left holes and she filled them. I had to find my place when I returned.

It's strange to see someone else's nail in a cabinet. I don't know how I see it but I do. I'm arranging the canned food. There are too many on the second shelf. I'm trying not to make it obvious. I have my patterns and my codes. And then I see the nail that isn't mine. There's a small invasion there. A questioning of who and when. I don't like to ask about it. I trust her. I've always trusted her. But someone else was in my space. It doesn't occur to me that it was her. That she may have made the repairs herself. I see someone take my place. I see her inviting someone to take my place. I put it away. I won't ever ask her. I was the absent one. She was only getting things done. Finding the balance without me.

I return to the nail eleven times in three days and then I decide it has to go. I'd like to take care of this when she's not around. I'm doing it for me and it seems gratuitous for her to know about it. There's nothing wrong with the cabinet. It's old but everything in the house is old. There's nothing wrong with someone having fixed it. There are other repairs from before we moved in. The nail is just like all the other nails. I don't even know how I noticed it. It's exactly the nail I would have used. It's exactly the work I would have done. But it isn't mine. And it cannot stay. I didn't mean to notice but I did. And now I can't stop noticing.

I check the toolbox for equipment. There isn't much I need. Just the hammer, some putty, a new nail. It's all there. I put it back in the box. Put the box back in the garage. Ready for when I get the chance. I'm good at waiting for my moment. I can calm myself as long as I can find the plan. She'll go to a meeting and she'll tell me how long she'll be gone and then I'll switch the nails and then I'll be home again and she'll never have to know and we'll never have to talk about it. There's something petty in my actions. Something unworthy of what she's been through. How she's kept the house together. How she's lived here for the both of us. I don't feel good about taking it away. But I have to do it and I can do it in a way that doesn't hurt. Or that only hurts me. I can protect her at least from this much.

I check the hammer and the putty and the nail each day. I know nothing is moving. I know they'll be there. I try to stop myself from checking but I find a way to do it every day. The most I can stop is from asking when she'll be gone. She doesn't have a lot of meetings out of the house. She used to go to the library for research, but now it's mainly on the computer. I don't know exactly when that changed. I was gone for it. That's how it is now. That's what works. But I can stop myself from asking. Wait for her to tell me where she'll be. It doesn't have to be a big window. I need an hour so I need two to make it safe.

It's six days from noticing and she tells me she'll be out on Tuesday afternoon. I feel the catch of breath. I try to pay attention as she asks if there's anything I need while she's out. If she can take me somewhere.

I take a minute. Pretend to think about it.

"No, it'll be good for me to be here. I haven't been here alone yet. I didn't even think about it, but it'll be good."

"Yeah, okay, that is good."

She nods like we're making progress.

"Let me know if you change your mind though. I can probably do it on the phone. But yeah, it's good if you want to stay."

I kiss her forehead.

"We're getting back to normal," I tell her, immediately regretting the lie. A step too far. Unnecessary. I should have left it alone. I should have stopped myself.

11.

I try to still the noise and everything around it:

There is so much content to attend to. So many details and piece for piece. I turn towards the smallest parts. Obscure the picture. Slow the frames. If I can keep us from arriving. Keep the road from stopping short. There are several things I know from here. How the view can change at any moment. How we do not have to know before we know. Also that the choices narrow. That words are part of what is real. And so I keep my silences. Caution her to do the same. Even as we find the places. Even as we name the names.

I don't remember time before this. Or I can see the general shapes. Before the breaking into pieces. Before the concentrated gaze. There's a looseness I remember. I miss it in the vaguest sense. Without knowing what it feels like. As if I was another person. As if every part of what I was is separating from the now. It's hard to travel forward. I know the steps and trust the road. But I do not know where I am going or how I will arrive or when. I try to concentrate but all I see are pieces. I cannot find my place inside. I cannot hear my footsteps.

There are tricks I learn to play from here. Everything can be a song. I pretend I am a metronome. I pretend I am a changing tide. Things fit better into fives. I pry them open. Stretch them out to fit my cause. This is also part of learning. How to shape the shapes around. How to keep the words from stopping. How to find another way to say. Something that attends the rules. I am getting good at it. I am getting practiced.

It used to fit inside me better. That was part of being five. Of understanding who I was and how to be it. Growing came to be a problem. It wasn't about stopping. It wasn't even about the numbers. It was something I tried. Something that worked until it didn't.

I'm hoping this can be the same. That there can be completion. I don't even know how long we're talking. I just want to wait it out. I want to wake up in a year or two years and I want it to be done with. I want to not remember all the details. I want to be ignorant. I want to be past the worst of it and knowing how to make things work. I want her to talk to me. I want the conversations to have happened. I want to not remember the first words. The first time she tries or I try. The awkwardness of words and actions. The silences before. The pauses between. All of this is somewhere in the future and I would have it pass me by. There is enough to deal with on the table. There are bombs and fires. There are injuries and illnesses. There are ways we work. Agreements that bind us. Illness is an honest room but we did not think to be here. When there is already damage it is easier to believe in the finite. That what has been sustained is everything. It is also the curse of the healthy. That the first instance is a head cold and then catastrophe. That nothing is to scale. I am charting new territory. We never thought to live here. And now I live here. And because she lives with me, she lives here too. And I haven't had the decency to tell her. That's the part that pulls me under. That there's something less than honest here. And still I cannot find my voice. Cannot find the words to introduce who I've become.

It's easier to find distraction. All the things that do not matter. I ask her about the neighbors. We prune the branches broken by snow and laugh about whether there'll be one more blizzard before the spring. We reexamine maps and plan vacations. I promised her a time away. I promised her recovery. That I only needed time to rest. And so I pretend that this is restful. I pretend to sleep and wake and realign my moments. We look at brochures. Talk about sun and swimming. Whether we'd like to be busy or alone. Whether we would like a crowd. How many people is too many people. How we would get from place to place. Whether things should be an adventure. If we'd like things to be easy. If we'd like things to be done. Some couples travel better than others. We haven't been a lot of places. There have been trips to see our parents. A honeymoon at the beach. There was a mountain trip before I left. We've always been at home here. Safest in our space. I don't know where this desire to be elsewhere is coming from. But I told her we could do it and now we will. I'm going to let her pick the where and I can pick the when. Or I can keep picking the when. Given that she would have had us there already. That we would have come and gone. We would be home and it would be past. Which makes me think I should have let her. I should have listened. I should have kept myself from speaking. Which is what I'm doing now. Every moment more silent than the last. More filled with what

I cannot say. It's beginning to feel like lying. There's an ache that I know is that moment of her asking what I'm doing. Of her looking at me and letting me see that she knows. I want it to have happened. I want the directions to reverse. Everything is forward motion. Everything is coming to a head. There's a release that happens in the aftermath. I can almost taste it. I can almost will it into being.

12.

Because we know we do not say:

I try to keep the actions small. I concentrate on the internal. Five breaths. Five swallows. Five moments between bites. It's too noticeable to make each sentence a five so I work with multiples. Keep things steady. Keep the count.

I let it get messier when I'm walking. I let the names start. When it's only strangers. Moving through the alphabet. This part is new. Last time it was all about the fives. I don't know if the names are good or bad. It doesn't matter. It's not a part of stopping.

It doesn't matter where I walk. It doesn't matter if the strangers see. But it makes it hard to get back in the door. To switch my rhythm. To smooth it over.

I'm almost home now and I see her in the front yard. Putting out new soil. Getting ready for the season. I try to remember the map I've made. I know I was at the park. I know I'm on my second alphabet. I haven't prepared for the intersection. I've got it down. Five steps for every pair of pavement squares. I see her see me. I wave. She waves and wipes her hands on her pants. She's going to wait for me to reach her. I have to change my gait.

I try to stretch it out. To make it four. The last one becomes an almost jump. I look up to see if she's watching. She is. I take another step. Onto the next square. This time I try for six. Which adds up. Which makes sense. It doesn't fit. Everything becomes compressed. I don't remember how to do this.

I look up and she's walking towards me. I know I should keep going but I don't. I stand in the fourth square since seeing. I wait for her.

"Hey," she says.

"Hey."

"Are you coming home?"

"Yeah."

"I'll walk with you." She pulls off her gardening gloves, takes my arm.

She takes a step. Now I'm one step behind. She's still holding my arm. I take a step to catch up. She takes another. I meet her. The third one hits the crack. Which is okay. And two more to get us to the next pair. I stop. She stops. She looks at me and smiles.

And that's how we make it home. Fitting my steps to her steps. Her fives to mine. And in the door.

C031390T

I hear them talking about what you were doing there. Why you were walking. I know I'm not supposed to hear. I don't say anything. I don't know if you'd want me to. I wish you could tell me what to do. I wish I knew if I was meant to speak.

Everyone says I'm getting too quiet. You never said that. Am I getting too quiet?

13.

Because it is already raining and already coming:

I hear her on the telephone. Canceling her day. Rescheduling according to the forecast. I should be outside by now. I should be counting and naming. Getting on. I try walking the corridor from bedroom to kitchen. There's only so far I can go with walls. I try to turn around. It doesn't work inside. I cannot fit here.

She's still on the phone when I hear the first wave of thunder. Ten steps to her office. I could have made it eight. But it's ten. I get there as she's hanging up.

"You okay?"

She turns around. Tries to smile but doesn't make it. She's looking at me when the sky brightens. She's not even facing the window. Maybe she sees it on my face. Maybe it's a reflection. And then she's gone. And then she's in the closet.

The closet is only two steps from where I'm standing. If I shuffle I can make it five. I give her a minute to settle in. Take my tiny steps across her office. Sit down on the floor. Lean against the brown door. Every other door in the house is white. But she didn't want to paint this one. She wanted to leave it how it was. How we found it.

"I'm glad I didn't go out walking," I tell her. I don't know if she can hear me. I've never asked if she can hear inside the closet.

"It's better when we're both home," I tell her.

There's no sound from inside the closet. Which is

normal. I've never heard her move. I've never heard her speak or breathe. I once sat here for five hours while the sky kept turning over and lighting up. She never came out for water or to get something to eat. I tried asking if she needed anything. Only silence. Only waiting. It felt like a betrayal when I got up to use the bathroom. I'm not as strong as she is. I'm not as focused.

"We're going to be okay," I tell her. "We're going to make things okay. I'm here now. I'm not going anywhere."

I count to five-hundred and by the time I finish there is sun through whiter clouds.

"I think it's done, honey."

I stand up. Press my palms against the door.

"I'll see if I can fix that drawer in the kitchen," and I leave her to her room. To her exits.

She doesn't come out straight away. I already have the drawer off the runners when I hear her.

"Hey," she says.

"Hey," I turn around. Hold up the drawer to show her the cracks.

"That looks great, honey. Thanks."

"Yeah, I think it's probably original. I think I can get it."

"I'm glad you're home Otis." She leans into me. Her whole weight. Her whole breath. "I'm glad you're home safe."

14.

Someday:

There's the day before you know and the day that you get there. The day I met her and the day I knew what that would mean. I saw her hair first. She was sitting outside and there was just light coming off her. When I tell her about it now she thinks I'm saying it like a compliment. But it's just how it was. The way afternoon is just more yellow than other times of day. And it caught her inside it and she just shone. I wish I had a photo.

We didn't talk that day. I just noticed the light and tried to go back to my book. I wasn't the strongest student. My eyes were always finding something else to jump to. I couldn't keep them on the words. Or I couldn't keep them moving across the words. They'd get stuck somewhere or move to something else. It was hard to keep my concentration. I had to work at it. Remember that I was reading. Remember that I had a purpose. So I pulled my eyes away from the light and back to the page. But I knew she was there. One table over. I remember her voice when she asked for the check. I looked up but the light was gone by then. I was lucky to catch it when I did.

I didn't see her again for more than a week. Which isn't that long. But I thought about her. How maybe she was more important than the words. How maybe I should have stopped myself from stopping. How I could have said something. I went back to the café. Not every day. I was careful with habits even then. But I went back three times that week. Which is more than I usually let myself be in the same place. Which is pushing it. It happened on the fourth time. It was morning and there was no light but I recognized her when she walked in the door. She seemed to be looking for something. I thought maybe she was looking for me. That maybe I was also light. But her eyes moved right over and behind me. She raised her hand to wave.

She was almost at my table.

"Hi."

She stopped. Looked past me at whoever it was she was here for. Raised a hand as if to say she'd only be a minute.

"Hi," she smiled down at me. I stood up to meet her.

"Do I know you?" she asked.

"No, I don't think so. I saw you here last week. You had light coming off your hair."

Her smile stuck, her head leaned slightly to the left.

"I'm Otis. It's good to meet you."

I held out my hand and she took it.

She nodded, "I'm Cat."

I nodded, still holding her hand.

"I have to meet my friend," she pointed behind me and waved with her left hand. I looked around and waved too.

"Maybe we could have a coffee," I said.

"Well my friend is waiting. Maybe another day," still holding my hand.

"I can wait here," I said. "I have reading to do."

She looked down at my book. She nodded, smiled.

"Okay," she said. "I'm going to go now."

She looked at our hands. Reached over with her left hand so now she was holding my right with both of hers.

"I'm going to go now," she said again. "But you'll be here."

It wasn't quite a question.

"Yes, I'll be here."

She nodded.

"Okay then," I said. I turned and waved to her friend again. Picked up my book, held it up for her to see. I don't know what I was saying. Maybe to take your time. Maybe to show that I had something to do while she had things to do.

I watched her walk two tables back to her friend. She turned around and smiled just before she got there. I waited for her to sit before I sat back down.

I don't think I opened the book for quite a while. I just held it. Looking at the cover. Reading the back blurb. Like it was something new. I remember looking around the café. Expecting to find the light. Not necessarily in her hair but somewhere. I knew it was there and I just wasn't seeing it. I tried to look in every place. I tried to see everything. Sometimes I heard a word or a laugh coming from their table. It reminded me I should be reading. That it might look strange to her that the book was closed. It occurred to me that the light might be inside the book. I opened it up to the first page. Words I had already read. The page did seem lighter, but not like last time. I turned to the section I was meant to be reading. Moved word to word. It didn't matter if I never saw the light again. I was going to sit here and when she was done she was going to come back. And then we would meet. And then I would know her.

15.

There are words we do not use to fill the air:

I was not without complications when we met. I was still myself, just loosely knotted. She knew my history as soon as it was safe to say. It was not something to hide or put away. I had been afflicted and now I was not. I was a brave child. A man fit for war.

She told me of the times between. The absent times. While I was tightening the knots and she was learning how to be alone. It was not the first time for either of us. She told me about learning to take up room. How she never did it with Tom's space but she had to do it with mine. How she was scared to memorialize me. How she lost Tom and she lost her home. How she wanted this house occupied and had to work twice as hard to do it without me.

Meanwhile I could feel each rope tightening. I knew I would have to explain them when I returned. I thought about preparing the space in some way. How do you tell someone trouble is coming when trouble is already here? Every time we spoke she told me she needed me to come home safe and I could not find the words to tell her I was failing.

We had already agreed on so many silences. I knew there was a closet and I knew not to go inside the closet. I knew that she went there in the thunder. I knew she didn't need me to follow and she didn't need me to rescue her. I knew she had been doing this a long time but I did not know how long. I knew she didn't want to talk about it. It was the first thing she explained. And I took her at her word. That's how marriage works. Mutual silence. Unfilled space.

My mother-in-law asked me about it once. She wanted to know whether we talked about it. She told me she always hoped Cat would grow out of it. That she hoped still, but not really. I wanted to ask her when it started. But even that felt like an invasion. If Cat wanted me to know she would tell me. If she wanted me to see the closet or the rooms that came before me. My job was to stand outside. To guard the silence.

I told her Cat was okay. That she was good at taking care of herself. She gave me a look like I was meant to be the one taking care. Which was true. Then she asked me why Cat did it. Which was how I knew I wasn't the only one Cat couldn't tell. Which somehow made it better and also scared me.

And then I came back tied in knots and unable to make the slightest sound about it. I felt her watching. Not exactly how my parents used to watch. But it did remind me. It's the way you watch someone when you want to know something but you don't know what you want to know and mainly you want them to know that you love them and will love them no matter what even if they're angry and especially if they're sick. I didn't like her looking at me that way. I knew it probably wouldn't stop if I told her. I couldn't loosen the knots, but I could show them to her. I thought maybe parts of the look would change. The angry parts. The questions. I knew I couldn't make it good but I could try to make it better. It was a step towards. It wasn't how we thought we worked.

I never expected reciprocity and I never got it. She was still exactly who she said she was, even if she said so little. I was the one who had changed my face, so I was the one who needed to reintroduce myself. I'd been home for twenty-five days. It was longer than I meant to keep silent.

She took it better than I played out in my head. She took it like a person who does not like to be questioned and so does not offer questions of her own. She let me tell her everything. She asked me what I needed. If there were rules for me and rules for her and which ones we could talk about.

The one thing she never asked was why. That was the main agreement. Not mine but hers. I don't think I would have minded. I've never had an answer and never sought one. I think the same is true for her. Except that she minds the asking. The first rule has always been not to ask about the closet. Even before not going in the closet. Even before not rescuing.

16.

Because not everything can fit into the space:

I group things together as best I can. There are leftovers and missing pieces. Imperfect scenarios. Imperfect days.

I try to do this invisibly. Which isn't possible. Not now that she's watching for it. Scanning the room for misplaced objects. Groups of five.

She tells me it's okay. That we can move things around to make it work. But it feels more private than that. Like I'd only be pretending if I counted with her. The numbers are for me. I can't share them. Even if she's right here. Even if she's telling me that she can help.

So I move the vase two shelves up. Line it up with the fifth book across. I count out the peanuts in the bowl. Make them divisible. Map out just the right amount of squares to fit each piece of furniture, each painting. I try to do this with minimal movement. I can make most of it work. I just have to spend time looking. Which is something I have.

It's strange to think about the space before. How I lived here without a grid. How I spent years moving over the numbers. Always aware but never falling in.

Sometimes I wonder if it's the same for Cat. That I was the uncharted space. And now here I am covered in divisions. All of these numbers pushing to the surface. Newly visible. Newly insistent.

17.

She should have said that they were coming:

Even without knowing all the contents. Even with my hidden frames. There are certain understandings. What she should have known. What she should have said. I know that I have bigger secrets. That I am keeping something still. That I am keeping something bigger. But it doesn't make it any better. She should not have opened up the house without my knowing. Neither one of us like surprises. We have our secrets. But that's about keeping things quiet. Not about opening the door to a parade.

I get home from the VA and they're in the living room.

"Surprise," they do not shout.

My mother, my father, Cat.

My mother jumps up and she's hugging me and I don't really understand she's in the room.

My father is standing in front of the couch, behind the coffee table. Looking at us. He looks happy. Happy to see me. Happy to see my mother hugging me. He walks towards us and puts his arms around both of us. I feel like I'm shaking on the inside. I'm not shaking so they can see. I don't know why this is so wrong. I'm happy to see them. I just would have liked to know.

"I didn't know you were coming," I say it to Cat. I say it over my mother's shoulder. Over my father's arm.

She's standing by the wall. She's already trying to fix things.

"Okay, okay, let's let him breathe," she's coming

towards us. Her hand on my father's arm, then my mother's. They let go.

"You didn't say," I try to say it friendly. I don't want them to know or her to know. I'm trying to keep things to myself.

"We wanted to surprise you," my mother. "We made Cat promise not to tell. You look so good. I thought you'd be too skinny." She turns to Cat, "He looks good."

And then we're all sitting around the kitchen table and Cat's making tea and I'm making coffee and my dad's telling a story about the drive from the airport.

I'm embarrassed that we don't have any cake. We don't eat cake and so we don't have cake. But if someone was sitting in my mother's house she'd definitely offer them cake and that would be normal. I look in the freezer in case there's something there. I look behind things and even when I know there's nothing there, I keep looking. I go back to making the coffee. I put the milk and sugar on the table. I go back to the freezer. I try not to open the door but I open the door. My mother looks up. Which is what I don't want. Which is why I want the cake.

"Do you need something, honey?" Cat asks.

"Cake. I thought maybe we had some cake," I say into the freezer.

"You want cake?"

"No, I just thought maybe we had some cake. Maybe we could give my parents some cake."

"We're fine, Otis. Really Cat, we're fine," one says or the other says, their voices overlapping.

Cat's face goes a little red. She knew they were coming.

She should have thought about it. She goes to the pantry, pulls out a box of cookies.

"Here, we have this. I'll put them out."

And she opens the box, starts laying them out on a plate. My parents are both looking around the kitchen. Trying not to see us.

Cat puts the cookies on the table, pushes the plate towards my mother.

"We really shouldn't even eat this stuff," my father says, picking one up. He smiles at Cat, "Just promise not to tell my doc."

"Your secret's safe with me," she laughs, but not really.

I bring the coffee to the table. A mug for my dad, and one for myself. Cat pours tea for herself and my mother. Everything's awkward now. I made things come apart. I can fix this. I can make things normal or closer to normal.

I put my hand on Cat's hand. She tenses then relaxes.

"She's such a health nut," I tell them. "The cookies are probably gluten free or something. I don't know what I was thinking looking for cake."

Everyone relaxes a little. Cat picks up a cookie.

"Gluten does taste good," she says, taking a bite.

"Do you remember our wedding cake? Who has carrot wedding cake?"

Cat pretends to look offended, "You told me you loved it."

"I told you I loved you," I kiss her hand, "Your desserts, not so much."

Everyone's laughing now and I can breathe better for

it.

"So how long are you staying?"

There are four of us at the table and I am trying to find a way to make it five. I am trying to make the objects add up or to make the objects a person. I am trying to do this without showing.

"Till the fifth," my dad says.

I try not to let it show. I know he would catch the smallest mark. I add it up, try to pretend the number is another number.

"So four days," I say. "That's great. That's fantastic. Is there anything you want to do? Anything you want to see?"

"No, no. We just want to see you and Cat. Just be here, nothing special."

And we're past the five. Just like that. There are four people at the table but things will change on the fifth. I can use that without showing. If I can get past the number without him seeing. Things can't be all that bad. I mean I know that they are. But not so bad that I can't hide it. Not so bad that we won't get through.

"It's good to see you," I say. Which is five words. Which I didn't do on purpose. Which I'll have to keep an eye on while they're here.

18.

Some of what happened before I was seven:

Five was my year. It was when I started to recognize myself in the mirror. It was when I was able to tell people who I was. Some of it I did out loud. I watched my dad shake hands and say his name and I did the same. I'd reach my arm out and up. Fingers and thumb at right angles. *My name is Otis*, I'd say. Counting it out. *So good to meet you*, I'd say. Keeping time like I learned in music. My mother would smile down at me. Run her hand across my hair. *My little gentleman. Just like his daddy.*

I learned to write my name. O-t-i-s-stop. Counting the stop to make it five. Mrs. Brown called it a period but period is too many sounds. It was a stop and I always wrote the stop. Even when I had to use it in a sentence and there wasn't meant to be a stop. Mrs. Brown would tell me every time. She'd write in green pencil on my paper. Sometimes she'd draw a circle around the stop and try to pick it up and move it somewhere else. But it was a part of my name. I told her it was the same as the other letters. She said it wasn't exactly the same. *Okay. But it goes there. With the other letters.* And she let me be.

I arranged things in pods of fives. They didn't have to be the same. They just had to belong together. It was possible to do this without people noticing. It wasn't a secret but it wasn't anything I needed to talk about. It was just for me. To make things mine. I was five and there were five places I could sit in my room. I was five and there were five books I liked to hear at bedtime. Five chews for a bite. Five sips for a drink. Five fingers on the door when it opens and five fingers when it closes. I tried to brush my teeth in five strokes but my mother wouldn't have it. I tried five strokes per tooth and it took a long time but it worked. She'd tell me to hurry but she didn't tell me to stop.

I knew how things worked at home. I knew how they worked at school. I knew the way to the park and all the signs and how to match my feet to the concrete blocks. Everything divided out over time and it made me safe. It made me a little gentleman. Just like my daddy.

The summer I turned six we went to the lake. The three of us but also the dog and also the lake. So that made five. On my birthday, my dad made blueberry pancakes for breakfast. I ate the first pancake in five bites and then I remembered I was six. I ate the next pancake in six bites but it didn't feel right. The last bite wasn't cooked right. It didn't taste the same. I told them I was going to eat six pancakes because I was six. My dad said that was a lot of pancakes but I sure could try if I wanted. He made them a little smaller and I polished off three more pancakes and limped through the fourth. I did each one in six bites and each time my jaw stiffened on that final piece.

Then there were words. Everything was a five beat bar. Everything counted out before I made the words out loud. And now I had to add a beat. Everything ended on an afterthought. I found myself finished and unfinished. Adding a *so* at the end of each sentence. *My name is Otis.*

So. So good to meet you. So. My name troubled me. I put a stop before the O but it didn't look right. I tried a second stop after the first. It didn't look right either. One day my teacher wrote her name on the board and she underlined it and there it was. The six. So that was my name now. O-t-i-s-stop-underline. And it worked but it wasn't the same as O-t-i-s-stop. The underline wasn't the same as the stop. It didn't feel like it was really mine. Really necessary.

It took a long time to brush my teeth now. I would watch the water in the sink and think about the lake. My mother would tell me to hurry up. She'd turn the water off so we didn't waste so much but I'd have her catch some first. Make a little lake in her hand or a little lake in the sink. And it would remind me to make the sixth stroke. To keep up with myself. To stay on track.

The biggest problem was walking. There were still five beats in my head and five steps to each piece of concrete. And so I would stumble on the six. On every six. Like a visible hiccup. That gap between who I was and who I was now. That failing bridge.

It was the walking that made them notice. Even more than the *so*. That I nearly fell at every sixth step. That I could not find my rhythm. Could not make a new song. I was so much my own when I was five. And some of me stayed there. Some of me stays there still.

19.

It doesn't do to stay inside it:

It could have been any number. I think that's true. It's hard to imagine attaching to a four or a six. But it could have been that. It's just a matter of timing. It's just a matter of who.

I should know more about the statistics. The odds on the odds. The evens. Whether a number is prime. The ease of counting. The space between.

I should know but I keep myself from looking. I know the dangers on the road. I know to steer around.

There are five wounds. Five books. Five sacred symbols and pillars. The third good prime. The fifth Fibonacci. I shouldn't know these things. I shouldn't let them distract me. How five can be the third in line. It doesn't work. I try to rearrange it but the details loosen my fingers. Weaken my grip.

There was another kid who was all about seven. I didn't understand him. I thought he was lucky to have the weeks. I thought he could find a way to make that work better. But he was always stealing fingers and toes. Trying to get them to add up. That's something I didn't have to worry about. Anatomy was on my side. That had its consequences later. The temptations of a hand. A foot. I try not to spend too much time on them. But they're all around me. Fingers and toes. Perfectly portioned. Counting out the space.

20.

Some of the things I do not show:

My parents look surprised when I suggest a game of scrabble. Even this many years later, there's something they're trying to protect me from. Home from war and endangered by letters and numbers. Which is absolutely true.

Cat sets the board up on the dining room table. We pick our tiles.

"It must be a lot to get used to, being back," my mother says as she places the first word across the board. "For both of you."

"The meetings at the VA help," Cat tells them, rearranging her letters.

"Oh, I didn't know. That's good. That's good they have that here," my mother.

"Yeah, it's really good. I went too when Otis was away. It's good to have a community, you know?" Cat looks at me, she wants me to come in.

I'm trying to make the letters add up to words. Trying to make it okay for the words to not add up to fives.

"It's your turn Otis," Cat says.

"I've met some good guys there," I tell them.

I let myself lay out a four letter word, three of my tiles and one of my dad's. Nothing adding up like it should. I don't know if I want them to notice.

Five breaths. Which I didn't think I'd have to do. To stop myself from counting, I start to talk. To lose my breath.

"There's a lot of services. Meetings to talk. Job training. Different courses. They help you if you want to take classes at the college too. And there's medical facilities. They have exercise rooms and physical therapists," they're all looking at me. My father is nodding.

"You think about going back to teaching?" he asks, his word adds up to twenty-five, double word score makes it fifty.

"Yeah, maybe. I was thinking about going by the school soon. Just to say hi. But the VA's good. I go to meetings twice a week."

"That's great, Otis. Maybe we can go with you while we're here. If there's family sessions or something," he rearranges his tiles, looks up for an answer.

"Yeah, maybe. Cat and I sometimes go together. I don't know if there are parent meetings," I don't know why I don't want to do this but I don't. It's better to say yes. To pretend that we're moving towards it and then to turn away.

"Country, twelve," Cat lays the tiles down on the table.

"Nice," my mother says, noting the score on her yellow pad. "Well it sounds like you're getting back into it. I can't imagine. It can't be like coming home after any other thing. It must be a lot to adjust to." She looks over her tiles. "They help with that too, yes? If you need help? They help with benefits and other things?"

"I guess. I mean we're doing okay. We saved a bit and Cat's busy."

"I don't want Otis to rush into anything," Cat says. "He's only been back six weeks. We're just getting used to things again."

"I go for walks now," I don't know why I'm talking. I want to take back the now. It feels like a substitute. Like a giveaway. I know it's my turn. I shuffle the tiles on my rack.

"Pass," I say. I make myself pick up only two tiles. Put them back in the bag. Shuffle. Redraw.

Cat looks over at me. I'm saying more than she expected. I'm making her nervous. Which I do not mean to do, but there it is. There we both are.

My dad takes his turn without speaking. He adds a d to ear. Five points. He's watching me so closely.

I don't know what to say now. I want to say more, not about the walks but to cover the now. I don't know how to keep this going. I look over at Cat.

"He goes for hours," she looks at me to check. I nod. "I love walking, but I don't know how he does it. The other day he was out, how long was it Otis? Maybe four hours? I'd be exhausted. But he's great. He comes home energized from it. Not me. That would do me in."

"Four hours?" my mother laughs, taking her turn. Earthy. Twelve points. "I was thinking of tagging along, but I guess not. You're too much for me."

"Me too buddy," my father. "You're on your own there."

And that was all we had to say. That was how she made it okay for them to be there and for me to be gone and be home again. For me to stay on this side of normal.

I just want time to let things settle. Maybe if they'd come next month. Maybe we'd have a handle on it. That's not true. I know I'm in deeper than that. Maybe they're here to make me say. I count my breath to calm it down. I play my turn. They don't know. Cat keeps her silences, but not my parents. Five more breaths. Cat is telling them about her gym. How everyone looks so perfect and none of the women sweat. She's got my mom in the conversation but dad's still on the outside. Still watching. Still listening. Pretending to calculate Cat's latest word.

I haven't seen him like this in a long time. So careful. It's almost like he knows. But I'd see it on Cat and on my mother too. If it was a conversation. So far it's just him and it's not knowing. So far I can work around it. I can keep us busy. Keep us talking. It's the pauses that get dangerous. So that's the plan then. Keep talking. Keep moving the pieces around the board. It's only days and it's only what we have to do for now.

21.

What I do to keep from counting:

I tried singing when it started. I tried repeating the ones. Turning back on the threes. It's all mathematics in the end. I would find a way to find it. If I turn at the three the fifth is the final. Up and down the scale. The quadratics of getting where I need to be.

Sometimes the system gets too intricate. The avoidance gets bigger than the thing itself. It's hard to find the turning point. But I can usually catch the aftermath. Readjust the rules to keep from stalling.

It would be easier to stay inside. To let the fives be fives. To let the names take over. It's not like it's an interruption. There's nothing I need to do that can't happen inside this. But it feels like I'm letting me down. Like I'm going back to before I was better. Like I'm a kid again. And not the grown up kid who kept it together. It feels like I'm the kid that worried them. The kid they had to watch and fix. I want to stay fixed. Or get closer to fixed than I am now. Closer to where I was before I left.

Mostly I don't want my parents to see. It's partly not wanting to worry them and partly shame. At first I thought it was one or the other. That maybe I was calling it worry but really I was just embarrassed. Or maybe I would be embarrassed if they worried. But it feels separate now. It feels like both are true. You get to a certain age and you figure your parents can relax. You're going to be okay. You've got a house and a wife. There are people looking out for you. But when things go wrong it's back on them. I don't want to do that to them anymore. I want to be easier than this. I don't want to take up room.

The walking helps to calm and cover. It doesn't keep me from counting but it gives me something to count. It's its own system. Step for step. I can keep my eyes where they're meant to be. I can't do conversations but I can pretend to listen. That's okay for some people. Especially when they're walking. They just want someone next to them. Someone making sounds, nodding, shaking their head. It's enough for them. It doesn't work with Cat. Which is why I tell her I need to walk alone. She gets too sad when the numbers take me. Even though she knows now. Even though she says it's okay. I see her watching me. Watching my mouth. I'm sure it isn't moving but I see her watching it.

It helps that I can make the rules. It helps that no one has to know them. But I also know I have to keep them honest. I have to name them and decide. Lanie used to keep a list. She kept it on a special page and when we found something that stuck she'd write it in. One time I tried to cheat because I saw the list had nine things and I wanted ten. I made one up and she asked me right away if I was just making it up to make it ten. I told her I was but that it was also true now. That it was a new thing and I was going to have to keep it so she might as well write it down.

"What it we try to not do this one, Otis?"

She was holding her blue pencil and the book was open to the page. I wanted her to write the number ten on the left margin. I wanted her to add it.

"You have to put it in. It's true now. I'm not lying."

"I'll tell you what," she put the pencil down inside the book, "what if I promise to remember and we'll talk about it next week and if we think it should go on our list, we'll write it in then."

I didn't like it. It felt like holding my breath.

I looked down at the pencil.

"It's already true," I said.

"That's okay, Otis. It'll still be true next week and then I'll put it on the list. I promise. Okay?" And she smiled at me.

Lanie always believed me. That's one of the things I liked about her. She always believed me and she never told me I was wrong.

"Okay," I nodded. I was good at waiting. It was something I could do in private.

"Should I tell you about it again next week?" I asked.

"If you like. If you want to."

And she did write it in the next week. Just like she promised. And I did have to make it a thing. Because I said it and then it was true. Because I said it and then I had to keep saying it. Keep coming down on the same note. The same rhythm.

I'm thinking about making a new list. It helps to be organized. But I also don't want to add things I don't need. I already know I'm not up to five. It's more bearable if it's just knowing. If it's not written down. I worry that if I make a list on paper I'll have to pull it up to five. I don't even really like to think about it that much. I know it could get me in trouble. It's enough to navigate the names and the numbers. It's enough to know what is and is not permissible on walks. I could play with the rules and turn the walks into three things. Turn the three into five. But if I can leave it alone. If I can try not to do this one. That's got to be something. That's more than I could do when I was younger. That's something to be proud of.

22.

Because each of them has a name and each of them matters:

I start with a new letter each day. Working through the alphabet. Walking it out. I remember the name of each person I meet. I notice streets that are named for people. At night I research. Practice pronunciation. Variation. I try to remember them while I walk. Picturing their faces. Finding their eyes.

I know it isn't good for me. I recognize the patterns. The repetitions. But this is where I live now. This is where I live for all of us.

Dania. Dani. David. Davida. Denoul. Delilah. Every month I loop back around. *Elijah. Elias. Ehmad. Ezekiel.* Starting again. *Faroud. Fatish. Fatima.* Always trying for one more than last time. Always counting out the syllables. The vowels and consonants.

I told Cat about their faces. How I tried to find their names when I got back to the base. And I tried again when I got back home. I thought maybe she'd be able to help.

"You can make a map out of anything," I said.

She put her hand on my cheek and I knew she'd find them if she could.

"Where were you?" she asked. Which we knew she shouldn't. And we knew I shouldn't answer.

I went down to the basement and got the hand-drawn map out of my duffle. Already marked with coordinates and dates. I brought it back upstairs and laid it out across her desk.

"I drew this the night of the explosion. I put it in one of your envelopes to keep it safe. They would have court-martialed me if they found it."

It's the only time I did anything like that. I'm not one for breaking rules.

I didn't ask again for two weeks. She'd see me watching and she'd smile and look back down at her work. My map pinned up on her board. Amongst all the other families.

I'd see her at her desk in the morning and I'd head out the door. Thinking maybe if I came across the name, she'd come across the name, and then we'd know. Most maps depend on magic. Most maps break across a border.

And then I came home from a walk and the map wasn't on the wall anymore. It was folded up on her desk. Like she was done.

"I don't know what the next step is," she told me. And I wondered what she knew. Where she'd been.

"We're looking for four people but we don't know that it's only four or even four or any other thing about them," she said. "Is there anything else? It doesn't matter if you think it's important."

I pretended to think. To not be disappointed.

"Maybe the door was red," I told her. But everything was red. Which made the door feel less than accurate.

"Anything else?"

I shook my head. She nodded but I could see it wasn't enough.

She kept at it for another week. On nothing more than a secret geography and a possible paint color. And then she told me she was sorry. That we could try again if I remembered something else. But I know that it is up to me now. That it is up to magic and making do.

23.

There is expected and unexpected loss:

I wanted to say reasonable and unreasonable. But I didn't. So there you have it.

When I decided to join the army, I put my hand on Cat's hand and I told her. Whole-hearted. I made sure she knew what she had to know. About the house and the papers. About me and her. I took care of things. I told her I had to go and I told her I was coming home. And I took care of things.

My first week in Kandahar, I saw a man lose his legs. He was running. I remember the sound and then the light. He was a torso. I didn't see where his legs ended up. It looked worse than dying. The separation of body from body. And I thought, *that's going to be me.* I recognized myself. I settled into it.

Memory is not linear. We catch ourselves trying to know. As if to change a memory by changing a future. As if they are different. As if they are questions.

I knew that my body was not my body. I knew I wasn't meant to come back whole. I didn't know exactly how but I knew I would live and I knew I would lose things.

He was the first one. I saw people disappear. I saw a sergeant turn a .45 on himself. But the worst were the guys who got ripped in half. Who looked like war and died before the showing.

If I'd known before I signed the paper I wouldn't have signed. I wouldn't have used one arm to sign away the other. We get trapped in the space between. Knowing and not knowing. Stopping and not being able to stop.

And then my time was up. They sent me home. You have to understand, I'd known it solid. It had been a long time since I'd thought of my future as a whole. And then I was just home. Just walking around. I'd get stuck in front of windows. Surprised by the symmetry of limbs. My wife would put her head on my shoulder and I'd watch my arm come around her. Try to figure out how I'd hold her if I was one of the other guys. Someone who looked like they'd been in a war. Who looked like their past. Maybe I wouldn't need the numbers then. Maybe I could be normal on the inside if the outside broke away.

24.

On the confusion of eyes:

There are wants that go unfulfilled. Wants we don't pursue. It doesn't lessen the desire. We mark it down as unattainable. Build the fantasy. Spend some time.

And so when I saw it on him. When I saw my arm missing from his body. When I saw him end exactly where I'm meant to end. When it was so precise. So misplaced. I didn't even know him but there he was being me.

I was at Camp Bastion visiting Mike. He was in and out of waking. In and out of knowing where he was. When he nodded off the second time, I turned to talk to the guy in the next bed. And that's when I recognized him. Lying there without my arm.

It was not a desire to harm. It was not a desire to alter. Just a recognition of what was meant to be and wasn't.

He told me it was an IED. That he was the only one that lived. That he felt lucky. He didn't look like he meant it but it's what you're meant to say. It's what you're meant to believe. He told me they were sending him to Walter Reed. That they were going to set him up with a prosthetic. Set him up with a desk job and rehab. I couldn't look at him and see the arm grow back. It felt like more damage. More waste.

I told him I was sorry. And what I meant was that I was sorry I did this to him. I was sorry it was him instead of me. I wasn't wanting to be in the bed instead of him. I wasn't wanting to be in the car. I just knew it was a mistake. And I felt bad for the guy. I felt bad for both of us.

25.

It's the knowing that worries people:

Or the pre-knowing. I was in a body and then I felt part of that body depart. I didn't know I was waiting it out. I didn't know it was coming. I was still in the befores. A confusion of time and space. What I thought was there was here. What I thought was past was coming.

Sometimes I see people gathering my words. They look at me like I made it true. Like I proved my point.

I came home with an arm and I came home knowing it shouldn't be there. I couldn't help but add them together. When you get home from a war you figure that your body is a solid state. If you sweat at night, you sweat at night. You figure it's going to be that way until it's not. If the first time you hear a helicopter you're okay, you figure you're going to stay okay. But sometimes it creeps up. It's hard to adjust to that. Like if you come home okay you've got no business complicating things. And I didn't come home okay. I came home full of names and numbers. I came home with an extra arm. There's no other way of explaining it.

I read about guys who tried to get it amputated. Who tried to make the doctors believe it had to go. Who cut themselves. I never did any of that. I never figured I'd make it disappear. I never figured I had to. It didn't feel right but I didn't need it to feel right and I didn't need it to be gone. I just got to not relying on it. Like when you sit too long and your foot falls asleep. You can still walk. You just walk differently. You walk like a guy who can't feel his foot beneath him. That's how I thought of it. There and not there. Mine and not mine.

26.

There are times I long for accuracy:

When I find myself cutting the frame. Moving one step to the right. Cutting the left. Me. As I am. More than me. The outline of a body. Mine and not mine.

We are born to this. Outlines that move. Genetic memory. Maybe there's a time before arms. I should know this. Investigate. Find the day that limbs sprout from torso. Or torso from limbs. Directionality is a factor. I understand the possibility of concurrence. But I cannot live there.

Sometimes I find myself in a place and do not know my path. Could not tell you the direction of my travels. But clearly I am in the there of here and there. The second place that is also the first. There will be a departure. Even if I spend every moment in stillness. That is the way of trajectories. And so I travel. Pause. Count out the necessary steps. Travel. Pause. Lose my way. There is a shapeliness I cannot name. I know the taste of it. How my tongue traces the back of my teeth and my feet follow.

If every step I ever took was placed end to end. I do not know. It is no doubt more than average. It is at least a nameable country. It is at least Afghanistan. Laid flat. Not accounting for the mountains. I should calculate the size of my foot. My average stride. I should make it particular. My country. My measurements. My map across the world.

Numbers remind me of the dangers of personhood. I

keep myself to myself. Promise myself a stopping point. A place of destination. Even unmapped it still exists. As true as any known thing. Like something you imagine before the finding. Independent. Yours and not yours. Made and not made.

I walk for the sake of stopping. I walk to make myself more human. To remove myself. To find myself. I walk because I have a body. Because my legs remain. Because they are mine and I do not doubt them. I walk for Mike and the guy next to him. I walk for her. For the young mother and her three children whose names I do not know and won't. Whose house was not a weapons facility. Who had a pot of rice on the stove. Who I imagine moving across a dirt floor. Who I hope were somehow touching at that final moment. I picture her standing at the stove. Salting the rice. The youngest one at her feet. Maybe crying. Clutching at her mother's leg. Wanting up. I imagine the other girl behind her. Playing with her hair. Playing mommy. Imagining her own stove. Her own lost baby pulling at her skirts. I walk for the grandmother. I walk for the aunt. I walk for the boy just in from the field. The boy with arms full of vegetables for his sisters. Arms full of promises he made his father. And how everything spills out in that single moment. I walk for the moment he falls to the ground. Given the ability to walk, I walk. Given that I cannot trade my legs. My lungs. My years for theirs. I walk in remembrance. I walk to find their names.

Each day I move through the alphabet. Move through every name I know and every name I conjure. Knowing that I cannot know. Investigation fails me and so I walk. Knowing that I might never get there. I owe them that. And me. And every future person. I owe us that. Repentance. Memoriam. Not a righting of paths. But a continuance. A persistence. To carry the weight and keep walking. Because I miss the time before this. The man before this. It's not that I'm trying to find him or think that finding him would bring me back. It's not that he's a better man than me. Just that he saw things and I saw things and there are intersections only we can find.

Everyone lost themselves. Everyone found some other way of breathing that they did not know was possible or necessary. Everyone had the gasp between. Dead and not dead. You and me. Actual loss. The names we know and the names we don't. Faces we try to remember and faces we cannot forget. There is so much room. I walk through it. Trace it with my throat. The open space. Where they live now. Where I keep them with me. Not safe but hallowed. A named loss.

And so I walk. I pack myself inside my body. Fit myself inside myself. Make myself accurate. Make myself remember.

27.

I go through the alphabet, counting dark:

Because in the midst of this somehow she is able to sleep. It takes me weeks to believe this. To believe her breath. At first I think we are simply quiet. That we have used up our words for the day and are now each other's silent company. I listen to her breathing. How she shifts her leg down the mattress. I imagine she is doing the same. Mirroring me. There is something comforting in it.

Once I understand that she is really sleeping, I also understand I am alone. It isn't a bad thing. Just different. It's a responsibility. I thought we were keeping the dark for each other. But it turns out I'm in charge. I don't know why she trusts me with this. Why she lets herself vanish into sheets and pillows. I'm not what she remembers. I'm not what she knew before I went away. But there she is, sleeping. There she is, knowing I'm awake.

She's always had an easier time falling asleep than staying there. A car door slamming on the street. A siren. Any of these send her upright. Blanket clutched in her hands. I try not to be the interruption. I lie as still as I can. Walk myself around imaginary spaces. Try to remember the names I do not know.

I start with the easy ones. The most familiar. I know these are unlikely. *Abigail. Agatha. Alice. Andrew.* I get them out of the way. *Anna. Arielle. Ariana. Aron.* I unclutter my surroundings. Reach back into distant conversations. *Abiba. Afsana. Akilah. Ameena. Ameera.* Somebody's mother. Somebody's sister. *Asalah. Aseelah.* I match up the letters. Make a pattern of the shape. I try to keep their faces in my mind. *Asra. Azeeza.* I move through the daily research. The possible spellings. Pronunciations. *Adela. Adella. Alia. Aliya.* I stay as long as I can before moving to the next.

Cat turns and for a moment I think she's still awake. A sudden exhale of sleep. And I'm on to the B's. *Baasima. Badriya. Baraki. Bareen. Bastion.* I know these aren't right. I know I'm not even close. *Belinda. Bianca. Bob. Bobby.* These don't come as easily. I'm more comfortable with vowels. With openings.

Cat. Catherine. Cathy. Charlene. Charmaine. Sounds that are possible in English. But another tongue gets lost in these surrounds. *Cesia. Chaman. Charikar. Chehra.* The last one I found in a book and have never heard out loud. I whisper it. Try to get it right. A glottal stop. An emphasis.

I try to give each one its due. *Deena. Dina. Dinai.* All of the possible combinations. No matter how many letters. No matter how many times I've said it before. I want to get to the new names. But I know I have to pass through the familiar.

Hayley. Harryette. Hasida. I know that can't be right. *Haadiya. Habiba. Hamasa. Heniek.* There was a woman called *Hila.* Two sisters, *Homa* and *Huda.*

I tell myself that I'll fall asleep in the counting. The listing. It never happens but I tell myself anyway. In case this is the first time. In case telling myself makes a difference. I know I'll make it all the way through. Each round takes at least an hour. I have the time. This might be the one that works.

Paula. Paulette. Penelope. Patricia. Stringing the string. Getting me back there. *Pam. Pammy. Pamela.* Picturing her face. Patching over what I can't remember. What I never saw. *Palwasha. Pareesa.* It's feeling possible now. *Parwana. Parwin. Pazira. Pooria.*

"Are you awake?" Cat turns towards me.

I try to keep my place. I was close. *Pazira. Pooria.* I try to keep them on my tongue. I tell myself I'll be able to get back here. But I know I'll have to start again. Back through the ones that never work. Back through impossible consonants. Blurred eyes. Fragmented memories.

"Otis?"

I place my mental bookmark. Though I know it will not hold.

"Hey, sorry. Did I wake you?" I know I didn't. I could not be more still. More quiet.

"Mmm," she's almost gone again. I run my hand down her hip.

"Go back to sleep," I say. And she does. The quick in breath. The slow release. She curls away from me. Leaves me to the names. *Pazira. Pooria.* I try to step back in. Try to find my rhythm. It doesn't feel right. I try to move on to the Q's. I can't think of a name. *Quenella.* I know I'm just making it up. *Querisa.* It isn't working. I'm going to have to go back around. I shouldn't start again. Not now. Not so far into the night.

I try counting the room. The vertical lines. The creaks and groans of masonry. I imagine the space into perfect squares. Across the floor. Up the ceiling. Some of the squares cross the threshold. Which doesn't work. I'll have to start again. Make them smaller. Make them fit. The second time I get a little closer. I know I'll get there if I keep shrinking the squares. I tell myself I'll get it on the fifth try. Which is cheating. Skipping over the possibilities of three and four. I do it anyway. I make it work.

There'll be light through the curtains soon. Not morning, just a turn towards the day. I close my eyes. Listen to Cat's breathing. My breathing. How they overlap and separate. Hers is slower. Which isn't true when she's awake. I slow mine down to meet her. To bring me closer to her. To bring me closer to sleep. This might work. I concentrate on feeling the mattress beneath my back. On staying still. On breathing out. I try not to see anything but red. I tell myself I'm almost there. I'm almost falling.

28.

Constitutions change and we with them:

I make lists. Rearrange words. Choosing and not choosing. Pulling something close. Pushing something else towards tomorrow. These are some of the things that move across: The number five. The placement of letters on a sign. The placement of park benches. The names of the lost. That I do not need fixing.

There are natural pairings. Numbers and letters. Benches and numbers. I do my best to separate them. I try not to lean into numbers that catch me. I try to choose the lost ones. Tucked into the weightless space. Invisible. Impossible to hold.

This should be a private matter. But it can move at any moment. I can be on the bench when the bench becomes a number. Or is revealed as a number. It is not the bench that changes. Things blur. I see them better that way. The squint of truth. Cutting the sun. I try to keep up. Make an archive of movement. This over that. Mine. Theirs.

It is the lost ones that send me to the door. That make this unchangeable. I know that hurts my wife. I did not need to live but I lived. My body was exposed to more than it could take. And I escaped. More than whole. My mind was exposed to more than it could take. And I am piecing it together. Counting out the handfuls.

I am the caretaker. I am the investigator. I do not pretend to the loss of those who know their names. I only do my best to join them. To hold a thread between us. To make it visible.

29.

Things I see while walking:

First it is necessary to leave the house. To prepare to be gone for whatever period of time might prove true. Food and water. Temporary goodbyes. Given the rules, I cannot know how long I might be gone. I always return to sleep. But the hour varies. And sometimes I return by light.

The door does not present a problem. That much is a gift. I keep to the path that halves the lawn. The first decision comes at the right angle of street. There are three choices. Left, right, or cross the road. Cross the road is a temporary measure. The trick is to put aside whatever happened yesterday. To avoid the question of repetition. To feel the lean. Everything falls from this. It is only necessary to continue. To turn or not turn. To sit at each bench. To count it out. To walk the names. The faces.

I see the way the air changes. The heat. The movement of individual blades of grass. When I was seven I would spend hours looking for four-leaf clovers. I made myself promises of their existence. My finger and thumb stained green. The imprint of thumbnail on index finger. Blood raised to the surface. My cousin could pick a four-leaf out of any field. And he never tried like I did. He didn't concentrate. I would cover the garden square by square. I would work for it. Be scientific. I considered the validity of constructing my own four-leaf. Of grafting things together. Making it true. But I knew it wasn't true. That adding a leaf would only weigh it down.

I see the making and unmaking of life. The movement of pollen. I see green tendrils grope their way up the fence. Stronger than they were the day before. I start to rely on them. To trust that they will not retreat.

I watch for any movement. Any change of light.

There are rules for everything: When walking away from the house, walk honestly. It is not necessary or even possible to map the future road. It is only necessary to arrive at a position from which it is no longer possible to see the house. Do not exit the house with another person. If it is necessary to exit the house with another person, part ways as soon as possible and always without speech. Check the windows for receptivity.

A window is more or less reflective depending on the circumstance. Rain is a factor. Time of day. Cleanliness. Sometimes I pass right through and other times I stick. It is also a matter of angles. The slightest change can lose or find you. Which is not to say that stillness is a safety. Or even a choice.

There is a point at which I recognize the return. It is less a question of proximity than memory. The knowledge that this particular requirement has almost seen its end. And that tomorrow is more certain for the close of day.

30.

In the nineteen weeks between there and here:

I walked everywhere I could walk. I wanted to go places slowly. To span the distances. It means something to be able to see what I'm seeing. To know it's a tree or a town. To identify. To keep a log of what I'm passing by.

Everything changes except time. I try to make it smaller. To think of the smallest increments and to move past them. I don't know anyone whose life was changed in the twenty-four hours or fourteen-hundred and forty minutes of one day. It's quicker than that. There's your life. Then one small instant. And there's your life changed. That's why I don't get on planes. I don't want to move quicker than I can move. I don't want to arrive before I leave. It's one of the new things. It's not a lot to get used to.

I can pick a direction but not a destination. I can decide to just head left. Or to turn down the street by the creek. One day I decided to climb the stairs behind the park but they don't go anywhere. There was a good week of following the trails into the foothills. But then I realized it was following. That the destination was implied. Cat would ask me to pick up the groceries or return a book to the library, and I would do it if I could make it there without making it a destination. I always took the book along just in case. Sometimes I'd end up bringing it back home again and having to take it out for a walk the next day and the one after that. She didn't like it but it wasn't something to fight about. She'd just see the book by the door and know we'd try again tomorrow.

One time she came with me. We took the first right and walked down by the dog run. She almost-paused at every corner. She talked about the day but not about the destination. I did not speak. Sometimes I would nod or smile. She let me decide where we were going. She took my hand when we passed by another couple. It felt weird to be walking and holding her hand. Not weird to be touching her, but weird to be touching her while I was moving. She didn't come again.

After I had walked most places around here, I started driving. I would drive to a different part of town and then get out of the car and walk. The same routine. There were new names in every area. Names I didn't have before. Cat worried I wouldn't find the car again. She said I should make the car the destination. To make sure I got back. But I can't do that when I'm walking away. I can't depart from my destination.

Then I started stopping at benches. I would stop at each empty bench and count to five-hundred. At first I stopped at every bench. But if there was someone there they'd start talking and I'd lose count and have to start again. It seemed impolite. To be counting when they were trying to know me. I would ask their name. Add it to my collection. Then I stopped stopping where there were people. Even at the empty benches people sometimes stop and want to talk. But I'm okay with that. If it's my bench I can count. I don't need to say hello or comment on the day or tell them how cute their kid is. I just count and when I get to five-hundred I get up and keep walking. Sometimes they give me their name and sometimes I miss it. It's hard to miss out on a name but it's harder to interrupt the count.

I try to avoid parks with rows of benches. People look at me. Bench to bench. Up and down. So regular. I don't know why a system can make people think you're crazy. A system is how you keep things in place.

One day I just kept driving. It wasn't a decision. Maybe I didn't find the right place to stop that day. I drove out to the canyon and then along the old road. All the way out and then left. I thought about stopping when I got to a big empty barn. I pulled over and counted to five-hundred. And then I kept going. I didn't stop after that. Just drove until I got home and when I opened the car door my legs were cramped and I couldn't get out right away. I sat in the driveway for a while and then everything was okay and I could walk again.

31.

What I do when I get to five-hundred:

The first thing I do is breathe out. Every time. I never know that I'm holding my breath. It's not like I've been holding it for the whole count. But there's always something to breathe out when I get there.

I put my right hand on my right knee. And then I stand up into it. Pick a direction.

I try not to look for benches. I try to make progress. Sometimes there's whole rows of them. I don't know why they do that. They ought to space them out. Think about when a person might need to sit again.

I avoid areas with numbered streets. On bad days I avoid houses but I'm mostly okay with them. I gather the names and try not to add up the letters. I do it anyway. I add them up and divide them in half. To find the exact middle. Whether the letters divide even or if one becomes the center. I feel more satisfied when they divide even. Leftover letters feel like mistakes. I can get stuck inside a sign. Especially if there's punctuation. As a rule I don't count the spaces between words. I push the letters up against each other. I try not to count the punctuation but it interferes. It's there. More there than spaces.

32.

How to walk away:

There's a space between want and need. People forget about it. Fall into it sometimes. It's something you can learn to pay attention to but it doesn't make it go away. Maybe it's like that with anything you're born to. A kid reaches for things they shouldn't. Things they want. Sometimes they get a slap on the hand. Sometimes a loud voice. Sometimes they get burned. That's not the problem. The problem is that sometimes they get what they want and it's all reward. That's when they fall in. They step onto that false bridge and next thing they know they're knee deep.

One of the counselors at the VA says he always counts to ten. No matter what's going on he counts to ten. If he wants to put his fist through something. If he wants to have another beer. Good or bad he counts to ten. And if he still wants it he takes it. It's still want. It's not like he thinks counting to ten turns it into need. But it slows him down. Lets him see what he's stepping into. Lets him take a good look.

There's a momentum to a life. Like the speed you need to keep a bicycle going. You can't stop at every little thing but you can slow down at the curves. Most everyone follows the road but it only gets you where most everyone is going.

I do the counting to calm me down. Sometimes I do it to decide and sometimes I do it to remind me. To make sure I'm still moving. I'm still here. On TV people pinch themselves to check if they're awake. But you can feel a pinch in a dream. I read somewhere that most dreams only last two or three minutes. I figure if I have time to count to five-hundred I'm probably awake. It's not foolproof. If you can show me foolproof I'll take it.

33.

There is a code to holding anything:

To naming a person or a bridge. To the order in which we dress ourselves. The questions we ask. The answers. There is a code for understanding when a thing is broken. Codes that can be given to strangers. Codes that are secret. Codes that lay themselves over us even as we try to move away. I fit myself inside them. Try not to touch the edges. Forget the borders. I want to believe in sovereignty. That I am my own. That I am choosing this. That I could be elsewhere or other or gone.

Not everyone can hold the form. The army worked for me. It was always going to. The idea of it. Of clean corners. Of standing in the same place next to the same person. Of call and response. Loyalty. It's the world I always tried to make. The world I tried to live inside and not be seen. And there it was. Visible. A training ground for moving through hours. Moving through countries. For remembering how to smooth my steps. How to keep up with the guy beside me. To mask the stumble.

The trouble was fitting my code to their code. I used to think I should have seen it but I don't anymore. I make more room now. I keep a list: what I didn't know and couldn't. There isn't any fault in that.

There's a line between loyal and stuck. I don't know if line is the right word. It's wide enough to live in. Wide enough to mask the horizon. To not know when I cross over. It's not exactly comfortable, but it's home. It's not exactly mine, but it becomes me.

So I had my code and they had theirs. I learned to fit my steps into whatever line was asked of me. I learned to smooth over the surfaces. But something always remains. A memory of stopping. A shiver I cannot name.

I started to notice things. What it meant if I was fifth in line. What it meant if an order was given in five words or five syllables. I started looking for messages in letters. How many words meant something was true. How many words meant I was missed.

There was a time when I was the sixth bed from the right and the fourth from the left. It was hard to sleep that way. It was out of my control but a man's no good if he isn't sleeping and I got to be no good. I woke up one night on the floor. One bed over. I don't remember getting there. I guess the body figures out how to get you where you need to go. After that I talked to Mike. I asked him if we could switch places. He knew it wasn't okay. That we could both end up with a whole lot of trouble. But something about him saw something about me. And he did it anyway. He called me his brother and slapped me on the back. It meant a lot to me. He never asked why and he never asked anything in return. But from that day he called me his brother and I called him brother too. That's how it is there. You make a family. You draw blood. Find the silences you can live with.

Other things I just had to get by with. Nothing I could do about where I stood in line. Nothing I could do about when I was called to jump or to run or to cover. But I always gave it a meaning. Fifth meant things would be okay. Not fifth didn't mean they wouldn't. Just that it wasn't sure. Just that it might be me.

There were four shots when Mike went down. Usually it was more than that. That's the only time I can ever think of a four. Usually it was too many and too fast to count. But that day it was four. Incomplete. Not like any code we ever heard before. He went down on the second. We were all still moving. All looking for the source of fire. The third got him again in the leg. The fourth shaved off Juan's right earlobe. And then it stopped. Mike screaming and Juan not even knowing he got hit and all of us crouched and ready and nothing to hear. Nothing to aim for. We stayed long enough to make sure it was over. Four guys went scouting for the sniper. One wrapped up what was left of Mikey's leg and another tried to talk him into not dying. Someone tried to help Juan but he wasn't having it. Wrapped a bandage around his head and said he had no use for what was gone. Even when he started to feel it there was no more than a wince. No more than a stiffening of his neck and a decision to keep moving. The scouts came back with nothing. Not even shells or a trace. Like it never happened. Like it was just us out there and the noise and dirt flying us into the ground.

34.

I was never one for groups or groupings:

I try silence as an option. Having said my name. Gathered theirs. I find the foreheads of the men around me. Rest my eyes on them. Stay in the room.

Twenty-five seconds pass in silence. I find the floor two feet in front of me. Lean towards it. Sit back up.

There must be a question. The expectation of an answer.

"I'm okay," I say.

And they nod. Like there is more to come.

"I'm okay," I say.

Someone tells me I can speak here. I can tell them something about myself. Something about how it was. I tell myself to count to five and that once I have counted to five I will know what to say. But once I get there I'm still empty. I know I have to break with the floor. I raise my eyes to the center of the room. There is an empty chair across from me and three guys over. I settle on that.

"I didn't come here to talk," I say. Five breaths. Continue. "Things worked for me over there. The order." Five breaths. Continue. "Even when things were all fucked up there was still an order." Five breaths. "An action that followed an action." Five breaths. "Now it's different." Five breaths. "You get up or you don't get up and anything can change after that." Five breaths. Continue. "Sometimes I get stuck deciding." Five breaths.

"Anyway. That's all. So."

They're still looking at me but I'm done. It's more than I meant to say. Twenty-four breaths. Someone asks me if I want to go on. I find my place on the floor again. Shake my head. That's enough for a day. That's a lot.

The guy to my left starts talking. I move my part of the floor slightly towards him. Try to settle the rush in my ears. The panic of them knowing. Of being in the room. I try to hear his words. Catching only syllables. Pasting them together. Inaccurate. Impossible. My right hand tapping my right knee. Trying to keep me in the room. Trying to make a place for people to move around me. To share this false geography.

I know it means a lot to Cat. I know she thinks I need this. A shared space. Communal memory. She knows these aren't my guys but she says it can still help. I've never not believed her before. But I'm here. It's enough for her to want this. The way her head tilts up just a little when I walk back in the house. Wanting something good to have happened. Wanting me to have found something. She asks me every time. Not needing me to tell her but looking for that loosening of skin that only she can see.

35.

Adrenaline moves through like a raid:

The thing they don't tell you is that you have to walk it single file. It's the negotiations that get you killed. You know it in your gut. When to run. When to stay crouched a moment longer. Even as someone's calling that they've got you covered. They don't have you covered. There isn't a cover big enough. Thick enough.

It's not too different from anything else. You know when to cross the road. When to wait or not wait at the post office. Sometimes you know you don't need to check out the noise downstairs but you do it anyway. Just to walk the line. Stack the deck.

There has to be a moment when you know they don't have you covered, but you go anyway. You go on instinct. It's not reckless. It's just knowing. It's feeling time slow down and grabbing it. If you wait past that moment, if you miss it, the line disappears. You can't walk it anymore. No matter how small or how careful you make your steps.

I knew I'd come home and Cat says she knew too. She says she would have changed things if she hadn't known. It wasn't safe but it wasn't reckless. It was on the line.

Most people don't mean to put themselves in harm's way. That's not to say they don't. They think the line is wider than it is. I get stuck watching traffic now. Watching a car swerve into the next lane. If you spend ten minutes watching the highway you'll see what I see.

People could do with being more scared on the roads. Most of them get by. They swerve and the road opens up to make room. People are always watching for others even if they don't watch for themselves. I don't know why that is. It doesn't make any sense. But it works.

36.

The moment before the moment:

There's a silence that happens right then. As a kind of introduction. You don't always recognize it. But you start to listen for it. You start to move a little more slowly. To leave some space between the words.

It's not something you can understand without being there. The first one will always catch you out. The second one too. It kicks in at a different point for everyone. And then you start to hear it.

We were outside the house. Less than fifty yards. There were five of us. We'd been in the area for a couple of weeks already so I'd seen the house before. There was a kid maybe five years old. Always running around with a dog. Two sisters. One maybe a year or two older. The other still a baby. He'd sometimes carry her around, strapped on his back while he ran around with the dog. It seemed like sometimes the mother was gone for days. Or maybe she was just inside. I never went in the house.

I think it was just the four of them. All of the men had been removed. It was true in a lot of places.

It doesn't make any sense. We were right there. Right outside. One of the guys said something about the dog. It was tearing up an animal that looked like it had died a few days before. We couldn't see what it was. Maybe a small cat. It was gruesome. The cat was definitely dead already. There was something just wrong about the whole thing. We talked about whether there was some way to get it away. But the dog looked kind of wild. And it was so thin. So we watched even though we were trying not to watch.

We heard the baby cry inside. Saw the dog raise its head to listen. Twitch its ears. Blood on its chin. And that's when the silence came. Less than a second. Then the blast. We couldn't see the house anymore. We dove or fell or somehow ended up on the ground. Heads covered over. Ears ringing from the bang. And then the sound of burning. Of wood catching.

The dog was running in circles. I didn't know how it was still on its feet. No one could come out of this intact. A ten inch patch of cat skin hanging from its mouth. It was letting out a high pitched whine. A keening. The circles got closer and closer to the house and then moved back out again. One of the guys called it over. It was shaking its head back and forth. Like it was trying to get something out.

We didn't speak for a long time. The one guy kept talking to the dog. Without knowing its name. Moving through the languages. *Sag. Spay. It.* Trying to calm it down. We didn't say anything to each other. We watched the house. Listened to it. Stayed on the ground for what might have been several minutes. The dog settled down next to us. Chewing on the skin. Still whimpering but quietly now.

There were two smaller explosions. Something going off in the house. Probably a stove. A lantern. Everything was fire. And two small pops inside the noise. Two bursts of oxygen. It started the dog off again. Running around.

Running back to the house. I thought for a minute he was going to go in. It was enough to get me up off the ground. I was shouting after him. *Sag. Spay. It.* Like it was his name. Like I could call him back to me. Waving the dead cat. Baiting him back. *Sag. Spay. It.* I just wanted to keep the dog alive. I don't know why. I knew everyone was dead but I wanted to save the dog. I wanted to keep one thing alive.

37.

I might not know I know and might forget:

Maybe he called towards the house for one of his sisters. Maybe she answered. Maybe his mother called him in for dinner. Maybe there was a conversation in which I could not distinguish proper nouns. It seems possible that the children's names were spoken aloud. The only one I can't imagine is the mother. I never saw anyone who would call her by name. She was her title. Her matriarchal place.

There may have been a moment when a single word echoed from the house. When he turned towards and I recognized his name. Identified him. A momentary knowing now erased.

There is the trouble of languages that pass too quickly through our ears. Given the vocabularies that house us. I knew how to introduce myself. How to ask someone their name. How to go through the basics of direction and command. I never used words with them. I try not to imagine where I would be if I had. Something else to turn over on my tongue. Some other distance to place between us. Also they would be closer and still gone.

There is the trouble of every other person. Of conversations. Imperfect memories. Incomplete stories. Maybe I haven't asked the right questions. Maybe I haven't asked the right people. It doesn't seem possible to be this anonymous. All of these names and all of this silence.

There are counts for the known and counts for the unknown. Counts for those on the inside. Counts for collateral. For us and for them. Counts estimating the things we cannot know. I don't go near those. I cannot broach the inaccuracies. I always add four. Sometimes five. Wanting to include the father. Knowing he might already be included. I remember the boy as the man of the house. But I want to know where his father was. I put them back together in my mind.

I tell myself that it matters. That I'm their witness. That keeping their faces is something I can do. Which is also ridiculous. As if we lived together in this tiny world. As if they belonged to me. As if the children didn't have friends. As if there were no cousins. No teachers. No aunts and uncles. Possible grandparents. Distant neighbors.

And here is the part I try to steer away from. That it is possible that the father was gone and then returned. Like I did. That he saw it from a distance. That he started running. That he let out some kind of moaning prayer. That he could smell the ash before he got there. That wood crumbled in his hand as he grabbed the doorframe. That everything had melted into itself. That he stood at the threshold. Fell to his knees. Vomited on the dirt floor. That his hands, his face, are covered in sweat and dirt and ash. That he somehow stands. That he moves through the rooms. Believing in the possibility of finding someone. That he calls out for his wife. I cannot hear the words he uses. That he calls for the girls. For his son. I can hear his sounds but I cannot fit them into letters. They are the sound of sudden mourning. I see him walk back outside. Holding a pot in one hand and a silver candle stick holder in the other. Hitting himself in the chest. Banging his head with the back of his fist. There is no one close enough to hear him. No one to tell him what happened. He went away to keep them safe. He told his boy to be a man. To take care of his mother and sisters. He taught him how to harvest the fields. How to look after the animals. He told his daughters to be good. To help their mother. To be nice to each other and to think about him. He told his wife the truth. That this was something they had to do. That she should give the children good lives. That his brother would take care of them. And that the boy was a good boy.

And here he is. Covered in remains.

All of them ash.

38.

What I remember from the moments before:

When I started driving for the names I taped a piece of paper over the clock on the dash. Also over the odometer. It's hard to have the speedometer exposed. I try not to look at it unless I have to. I try not to let it matter.

I have a new CD I'm trying for research. I told the librarian I was looking for names and she smiled and asked me when we were due. I told her soon. And she took me over to the audio books. Showed me a CD of baby names.

Sometimes there's a name I haven't heard. A new pronunciation. I listen to the letters. Pause. Try to recite them back. I'm in the G's when it starts to rain.

I keep going through the H's and then the sky darkens. *Hadar. Hadassah.* I say them aloud. I think about heading home to check on Cat. I don't know where I am exactly. *Hamad. Hassan. Hateya.* I know that I should turn around. It's against the rules but I do it anyway.

When the car starts to slide I think about reading somewhere that those first minutes of rain are the most dangerous. That they leave some kind of coating on the road. I'm about to hit a pole. I pull the steering wheel left. *Iago. Ianna.* Keep pulling. *Ibrahim. Ibtesam.* I'm all the way around now. Facing back where I was before turning. And there's a tree instead of a pole. *Ichabod.* And then it's dark and light and I can't see anything anymore.

This is compression. All I know is thunder and names beginning with J. Somewhere there are sirens. Somewhere there are lights.

39.

Sometimes you can see the danger:

It wasn't hailing. The clouds weren't green. There were no funnels. No wisps climbing down to grab at the road. It was just rain and I just needed to get home. Needed to stand outside the closet. Let her know that I knew. That I was back.

Everything was different with the counting. It wasn't what she signed up for but here we were, moving through. And she never faltered. She let me keep my secrets. She let me tell when I was ready to tell. She let it be normal. Even though it wasn't. Even though it changed everything for both of us.

Storms are my chance to be the hero. That was always true but it used to matter less.

I thought about it while I was away. Especially in the summer. That there could be a storm at any moment. That she could be anywhere. That I could be anywhere. That I wouldn't even know about it. I can't exactly separate it from the counting. It all happened through the same window. I came back different and she let that be okay. I never thanked her for that. I never said the words.

That's what I do through the door. Let things be okay. Let her know that we can call it normal.

I was just going home. Now that I could. Now that I was.

There is danger all around us. I try to control it with the numbers. She tries to control it with the closet. We've already lived through our war. We've already survived. You don't expect to go off the road after that.

40.

The last and next thing is a light:

And so the moments collapse into each other. I am in the car. Everything is wet and bright. I am on a table. I am upside down. There is a cold metal clamp around my arm. Squeezing. Impossibly tight. I see my mouth opening. Making the shape of a scream. Instead the sound of a chainsaw. It is no longer raining. There is no more thunder. There are wheels moving too fast on linoleum. Fabric tearing. Ice pouring into buckets. Numbers and instruments. A stream of commands.

All of this fragmentation. All of this colliding like so many atoms. The car is on the table. The road is upside down. Fluorescent tubes splinter with the impact. A steady rain of latex gloves and voices. Something is holding me down. A seatbelt. An arm. I should have been home a while ago. It's already late. It's already stopping.

There is some kind of liquid. I'm colder than I should be. There are too many voices. I am alone in the car. The CD is no longer playing. I can still hear the back and forth of windshield wipers. It is no longer raining. I should turn them off.

It is too light for this time of day. The papers are no longer on the dashboard. There is no dashboard. There is a steering wheel pressed against my neck. Like a knife. Like a warning.

41.

This is what I've learned about absence:

There is carpal and metacarpal longing. Scaphoid and lunate. Twisted metal. Blue smoke. Hamate and capitate splinter into seventy-three new and unarticulated bones. The taste of gasoline. Glass and pillows. There is also this grouping of lost phalanges. Distal, middle, proximal. Each one plucked from my hold. Palm scored by half-moons. Lights and lights. First a voice and then a siren. The sound of cutting. Ulna.

I am coming limbless. Less whole than discovered. Picture a skeleton. Picture mine. Subtracted.

This is a magic trick. The fact of a fist. Something which might break windows or cheekbones.

I(t) will not unclench.

42.

We are not capable of hearing:

Maybe I am inside the closet. Maybe this is what it means. To be inaccessible. To be cushioned from the world. Unexposed to the flashes and rumbles. To not see. To not hear. To be distanced from the present. From the minutes or hours since entry.

There is no time here. I used to ask how she knew to come out again. If she could hear the end. Or feel it. She said it was something like knowing but without thinking. And I wonder if it will be the same for me.

Here we are in our bullet-proof vests. Here we are in our cones of silence. Waiting to know. Waiting to wake.

C081489T

I tore the other letter up and threw the pieces in three different trash cans. I thought I'd be able to give it to you but there's always someone in the room. It isn't safe. I'll write you another letter when you wake up.

I keep telling them you can hear things. They think I have a big imagination. You used to say that too.

Wake up.

I have things I have to tell you.

43.

When my tongue is almost capable of normal I say: "Here." As much to myself as anyone else. I do not know the room or the people in the room. I gather clues and assumptions. I hear the up and down of oxygen. *Shhh Shhh.* And I wonder if I called out before I woke. If I am being soothed. *Shhh Shhh.* If I was more capable of speech while I was sleeping or unconscious or whatever this halfstate was before thought. "Here." A question. "Here." A resolution. "Here." A reassurance. A comment on geography. On bodies. On bringing a person to my side.

It is not possible to know volume. To know whether a sound is happening outside my ear or in. "Here." Nothing changes. Uniformed torsos float. A series of steady beeps. More than one heart rate. More than one blood pressure monitor. I can hear a bag being taken from its hook. The empty pop of plastic as it releases. The heaviness of new fluid in its place. An ice road of saline from inner elbow to shoulder. "Here." This time I feel my tongue move. Not enough to know that I have spoken. But enough to know that I am closer. Enough to know that if I keep saying it someone will stop. Someone will smile down at me. Touch my forehead. An acknowledgement of possible failures. The slippage between here and help.

"Here." The smell of infection and medication closes my mouth against me. I recognize a wetness on my left ear. I try to raise a hand to it. To feel for the warmth of blood. The cool layers of gauze or plastic. Nothing moves. I try to shift my head against the stiff cotton of pillow. Nothing moves. Only blue and white torsos. Lights and machinery on wheels.

I concentrate on moving my tongue inside my mouth. On swallowing. On preparing myself for speech. I think my eyes are open.

44.

Getting born is an achievement:

All that time housing you. All that time walking around with one hand touching you through her skin. Talking to you. Letting you know where you are. Where you're going. Who the other voices are. Making you a home.

Learning to stay put when you're meant to stay put. Learning how to make your heart beat. And then knowing when it's time. We spend the rest of our lives looking at clocks but we know when to get born. I was five days late according to the schedule. But I was right on time. Right where I was meant to be and when.

My first death was temporary. The chart says ninety-four seconds. I count it as three days. The day it happened and two days of medicine. Of putting me back under. I could hear the same muffled voices. Like how women put headphones on their stomachs. I believe in that now. That's how I heard everything. Through bandaged headphones. And there was movement I couldn't control. I remember getting carried around just like the first time. Someone put a hand on the layer between my skin and theirs.

The first time the doctors chose a date and I waited them out. I took control. This time it was theirs. They kept me from me. They kept me two days away from getting born.

45.

It was always possible to see the years:

Undiluted movement. That she would stay and I would stay and how far that was from here. We were built for this. For eyes and skin and blood that will not keep. We made promises. Scattered want. Not to lose but to make it grow. To mix it with our particular genetics. A birth of attention. The before and after of crossing bones.

Before I woke up I saw her face. Even now I cannot say if I could hear her. "I'm here," she did or did not say. And it moved through skin and air. Through packed gauze. Betadine. Morphine. Fluids in and fluids out. Something keeping me asleep. Something moving my lungs. All of this fluorescence. And it is her I see. Her sitting on the bed. Her in the garden. Her with her hand moving across the page. Writing me letters. Bringing me home.

One of the first things I learned about her was that thunder made her hide. The first rumble would send her to the closet. If there wasn't a closet there was something else. A bathroom. The floor of the passenger seat. She had various strategies to move through streets. The first recourse was to find her way inside. A shop. A restaurant. An apartment lobby. The strangeness of it was enough to convince anyone. She would enter and announce her need to stay until the sky was silent. No one argued with that. No one refused. Inside was only the first layer. There would need to be a changing room. A bathroom. A secondary wall. Inside inside. Even in the absence of structures she found a way. Building a cave of clothing. Of hands over head. Of smaller and smaller and disappeared.

One of the second things I learned was that she was not ashamed. She knew that other people did not collapse into themselves like this. My little black hole. My dying star. She knew that even if it was only her, it was still true and necessary. That maybe she didn't breathe like other people, but still she breathed. And so it was possible to be her particular self. To be wanting and not want. To sink into the warp of it.

Because it was a part of her it became a part of us. She didn't need me in the closet. But I needed to be outside. I needed to be the next thing. To be as close as I could without joining. I wanted to create a world in which there was just one wall between us. I learned to still myself. To occupy the space beside. Regardless of surfaces. Of time.

A shared geography got us this far. And then I left. My sky wasn't her sky. My morning halfway through her day. At least the winter months were safe. But once we got to spring, every silence was filled with possibility. She is braver than I am. That has always been true. She went to her closet. Her secret wall. And I could not find her. She made herself safe without me. I was the one who got stuck. Who painted clouds on the ceiling and opened them. Knowing it might be now. It might be happening.

46.

Conversations slip and then they stay:

My name is a trigger. I don't remember everything but the words always start with my name. Cat telling me what the doctors told her. Telling me what they're doing when they come to check.

"Otis, they're going to change the dressings." All of her breath exiting. I want to tell her to look away. That she doesn't have to watch. That I can't feel what they're doing but I can feel her stomach turn.

Sometimes she talks about me. Asks the nurse a question. Speaks to her parents on the phone. Tells my mother something before she leaves the room. It feels like eavesdropping but I don't know how to turn it off. I learn that my fever spiked but it's steady now. I learn that they're worried about the skin flap but I don't know what that means.

She always says goodbye before she goes. Even if it's just to the bathroom or the cafeteria. At least I think she says goodbye. I just hear the name and what comes after. "Otis. Don't go anywhere."

Sometimes it's just my name. The last word in the sentence and so the first to come through. I wish there was a way to make her start again. To get the order right.

47.

A thirst that feels like choking:

And then my eyes are open and I am in a room with checkered ceiling tiles. White on white. There is no sound. No. There is muffled silence. No. My ears come into focus and there are voices but not here.

I try to look around without moving my head. A sharp pain stabs through my right eye socket. All the breath goes out of me. An almost cough. A rasping through tubes I did not know were there. I breathe out again. Trying to get closer to speech. To asking for water. For ice. Another almost cough. And then they are here.

Cat on my right. A man who must be a nurse on my left. They look down at me and then up at each other. Cat is saying something but I can't follow. I try to watch her lips. My eyes water with the effort. The nurse is gone. And then back. I am looking at Cat. Swallowing. Trying to tell her that I'm thirsty. Trying to make her see.

The nurse says something. And it looks like Cat says no. Everything turns soft again. And now I'm more tired than thirsty. I let my eyes close. Let the room disappear.

48.

This is also true:

Some of us get stuck in illness. Some of us violence. Some of us worry about machinery. Weather. Some of us fear a gradual decline. A sudden disappearance. Some of us hope to be in company. Some fear an eventual witnessing. A catalog of belongings. A patching together of who and what and where. Some of us try not to think about it. Some of us believe in other times and other places. We do what we can to move through the days. To make them possible. To make them ours.

We have our ways of understanding. Some of us with hands. Some with mouths. Or ears. Some of us with eyes. Some just know a thing to be true. Capture it in air and there it is. I have always had a fascination for shapes. Fitting myself inside them. Fitting them to me. It's a tactile experience. It is too much to think that any one thing is already perfect. We need to hone the edges. Allow for growth or dissection. Not because the thing is wrong but because it isn't ours yet. We have to earn it. We have to make it right.

I didn't make the car go off the road. I didn't fantasize the hospital bed or flickering yellow lights. I never heard an ambulance and placed myself inside it. I never ran my index finger along a blade. I knew I wouldn't go back. Even though it was meant to happen over there, I knew I wouldn't go back. I thought of it as a skip in time. Something was meant to happen. It didn't. I didn't think to look for reversal or replay. I went to the next thing. And on and on.

I never said the words out loud. That the arm wasn't mine. Not even to her. She noticed things. When it was absent. When I turned to reach for her in a way that didn't seem quite right. A certain neglect. But she never asked the right question. I never told. I didn't know the words. How do you tell someone that your arm is not your arm? How do you make the words make sense? Silence is more accurate. It doesn't make it any less than true.

I didn't know it was gone straight away. That's the thing about preexisting absence. Every part of me sunk into sheets. Clouded. I could not open my lips. Move my tongue. It took a long time to come back. I don't know if it was hours or days. Someone else was in charge of time. I was a passenger. I was pushing my way through but I wasn't driving. I couldn't see the road. I don't mean to complicate things. This is just a metaphor.

Not all of me came back together. My limbs lingered in the elsewhere. All of me was cold. I was aware of my throat. The feeling of corrugation. Dry cardboard. I was aware of the thickness of my tongue. A heaviness of my head. It ached but it was a dull ache. More a warning than a pain. It was telling me to stay as still as I possibly could. It was telling me not to make this real until I had to. And so after the first flicker I closed my eyes again. Took my moments.

There are categories. Intentional. Not. Accidental. Not. Most of us fall between. Wanting and not wanting to act. Knowing and not knowing how. It doesn't make it any less real. The slippage. It doesn't make it bearable or some kind of relief.

There is a four by six flag draped over the end of the bed. As if to tell them who I am. Who they're changing the dressings for. What I did to get here. As if to make a shortcut of everything that happened in between. I was A and then B happened and therefore C. As if A and B were not divided by countries and time. As if my C was their C.

I see the shape of my legs beneath the flag. Metal bed frame. Everything muffles but there is always this sound of feet moving through hallways. Rubber soles. Whispers. Doors that swish open and closed without ever clicking into place.

It takes time for a body to return. Some of that is medicinal. The slow drip of consciousness. I remember pushing up against the sides. Pushing out against skin. From the inside. Trying to find out who was there. I knew I was okay if she was in the room. The smell was one of medicine and disinfectant. Also of infection. Dried blood. But somewhere there were lemons and chocolate. So there she was. Before I could see her. Before I could know.

They tell me there was an accident. They ask me if I remember. Everyone is in uniform. Everyone is official. I tell them there was an accident. I can't make all of the words. The c's stick in my throat. Closed against the anesthetic.

I see her hand just above my right ankle. I see her

holding me and so I know I'm there. There's a moment in the midst of waking when I feel her hand but I cannot feel my leg. She is more real than me. More solidly in the room.

49.

There is an order by which a person is meant to heal: I know when to wake up because she tells me. "It's time to wake up now. It's okay to wake up now. I'm here." And I feel myself starting to move through the jungle. Blindfolded. Feeling for the voices. Catching myself on catheters and vines.

They ask me if I know where I am. I do. I can't make the words. I try to nod. To tell them with my eyes. They tell me where I am. How I got here. That I am lucky. That I am strong. Cat's hand on my calf. Telling me I am here. She is here.

People in uniform check the machines. People in uniform lift the sheets and examine every part of me. People in uniform ask me if I had been drinking. They ask me about prescriptions. They tell me that often people who have been in a war think about suicide. They ask me if I thought about suicide. They tell me they believe me. They ask me where I was going. How long I'd been driving. They ask me about my time overseas. They ask me how I'm feeling today. Whether I'll eat something. If I want the curtains open. They ask how long I've known my lovely wife. They ask if I want them to answer the phone. If I can hear it ringing. They ask if they can read to me. If I want company. If they can change the channel. They ask me to give the pain a number. One through ten. They ask me to give it a color. I give it red.

They call a conference. An accounting of what is lost.

I am a contusion. I will heal. They use the word *crushed.* They use the word *clean.* I can't fit them together. But they keep colliding. *CrushedClean.* They say there are options. Things to talk about later. Now is for healing. For growing skin. *Getting accustomed.* I ask for a mirror and they tell me to wait. I ask my wife and she pretends to look in her bag. I try to catch myself in the reflection of the IV stand.

It takes weeks to make skin. Even the smallest paper cut has to close over. Things happen in the meantime. There are pamphlets. Exercises. Information on how I should feel and who I should talk to.

They tell me about body-powered components and prehensile devices. They tell me about support groups. The various levels of cosmetic restoration. They tell me about the golden period. Before the neurons reassign. They ask me what I can feel.

"Everything," I say.

And they nod like it's a good thing.

The first time I say no they understand.

"It's a shock," they say. "It's a lot to get used to."

And they leave me alone. Leave the pamphlets on the table. The second time they send a counselor. He tells me I deserve to be whole.

"Okay," I say. Meaning that I am. Not the parts but the sum.

He says he'll send someone to talk it through.

"It's okay," I say.

Which he takes as agreement. He leaves the pamphlets. I tear out all the legs for Mike. I tuck the rest under my lunch tray and they take it away with the cold potato soup and saltines. There will be more pamphlets once they know they are missing. But for a few days they'll just be gone and no one will try to replace them.

50.

This is to that:

We're full of mathematics, you and I. Handspans pressed forehead to chin. Circling a wrist. Measuring. Crown to pectoral. The width of the shoulders. Shin bone.

1.618 inches from where I end. Exactly the length of her thumb and significantly smaller than mine. Sinew and skin. Incomplete muscle. Colder than it should be. Overexposed.

None of this happens while I am awake. First there is a tear and then a cut. And some small part of me is left between. A thumb's worth.

51.

Conversations change when they move through the door:

Inside there is a tone of certainty. Of perseverance. Sentences move their way upwards. As if searching for that highest point of hope.

On the other side of the door everything flattens out. I can rarely hear the words. But there's a rhythm that steadies and holds. Gaps and whispers join together. Everything becomes unpunctuated. Harder to define. To locate the exact meaning. On the other side of the door things are more unashamed. More comfortable with ambiguity. But I cannot get there.

On the fifteenth day I hear an ice cream truck and remember that there isn't just outside the room but also outside the hospital. That isn't exactly true. I was always aware of other countries. Of roads and houses. But I become aware of the pine tree through the window. Of the birds that pass through. I imagine pathways and benches. Families sitting together. The occupants of this temporary home. I learn to recognize the cumulative sounds of visiting hours. Engines and doors. Overbright laughs.

A few times I hear things that don't seem right to hear. A private loss played out in public. I try to let it move past me. Remind myself it isn't mine. It isn't me. Sometimes I hear things it isn't possible to hear. Things that haven't happened yet. I don't talk about them. I learn to make a place for them. To notice what I notice. But not to say. Chronology is personal.

Conversations take place around me. I listen for the undercurrent. I don't mean to be evasive. I trust the questions and I do my best to answer them. But that's only one layer. There is also the unaskable. The narrowly avoided. The said with eyes. The cannot think to make the question. There are reassurances of hands. Silent vigils. The position of a torso in relationship to another torso. I learn a lot by watching whose shoulder touches whose shoulder. By watching who looks towards the door and who looks towards the window. I try to hear all of it. To sharpen the lines of the people around me.

Sound is different in a hospital. When I was nine years old my cousin lived in a hospital and never came out. He used to keep the television on mute. It was always on. Always flickering. A place for him to put his eyes. A reassurance. One time when I was visiting HR Pufnstuf came on and we turned on the sound. It came out of the little control box. Like we were at a drive-in movie. We were both in the bed with the sound box between us. Everything smelled like plastic and the television voices crackled so softly we had to rest our heads together and lay them down right on the box. Like we were listening to a secret. We made our own world. Our own drive-in with popcorn and soda and no one to tell us who was sick and who couldn't come out to play. When our parents came back they stopped at the door. Like we were doing something they hadn't seen before. Like they couldn't decide if we were good or bad. We didn't know if we were in trouble. If I wasn't meant to be in the bed. If we shouldn't have put the sound on or maybe if we'd broken something. We waited for them to tell us something but they just watched. And so we kept our heads down on the sound box and laughed at Witchiepoo getting hit on the head with her own broomstick.

The hospitals overseas were different. I never needed anything more than medicine for an ear infection or a couple of shots. But there was always someone to visit. Someone to spend time on. Most people tried to get in and out as quick as they could. If you were there long enough for visitors it was serious. Usually it meant you weren't coming back. We'd stop in to say goodbye. To play a game of cards. To swap stories or jokes. To start figuring out how to know each other outside of this.

There is a code to living in a hospital. To growing larger than your chart or your machinery. I am learning to stop them in their tracks. To make them linger. To have them ask me how I'm doing and pause long enough to hear the answer.

I have a button I can press for Morphine and a button I can press for Help. I ask for a Do Not Disturb button but they don't have them here. Doors are built to swing in a hospital. Entry and exit. Unobstructed. Quiet shoes move in and out of earshot. Unanticipated hands. Whisper-Stories.

52.

It's hard to know time or even days:

There's always a clock but the hours move without meaning. I tell day from night by the nurses on duty. It's more reliable than windows. More reliable than waking or falling asleep. When the morning nurse comes I know that it's time to start again. To have a day. I keep at it for as long as it takes. Through meals and exercises. Through drugs that make it night again. People visit and I call it afternoon. Sandwich and soup means lunch. A hot meal means dinner.

There's a kind of interrupted quiet for the hours we call night. Voices through the hallway. Doors opening and closing. Sometimes a telephone. Sometimes a series of high pitched beeps. An alarm. A calling to attention.

I watch the clock. Try not to hear its movement. At some point the light will start to come through the blinds. We won't call it morning. Not yet. But we'll get a little closer. One more day under our belts. One day closer to home. To normal.

53.

Without knowing that I'm speaking:

I wake up from a sleep that I cannot identify as night or day. Three syncopated flashes followed by the rumble. I look around the room for Cat. Try to remember if she was here before I fell asleep. It must be night because I cannot push all the way through the medication. Cannot find myself completely. I press the button for the nurse and wait. Unrushed footsteps. Open door.

"What's up, hon? You in pain?" she walks over to my machinery. Checks the numbers and the chart.

"I don't know what time it is. Is my wife here?"

"It's four o'clock in the morning, hon. Nobody's here but us," she looks at me. It's always the machinery first and then me. I'm getting used to it.

"My wife doesn't like thunder," I say. My voice slurred. Something I can hear but cannot change.

"Uh-huh. Now you go back to sleep. You need something to help you sleep?" she pats my shoulder. Five taps. It calms me down.

"She hides in a closet. She has a special closet. Just for storms."

My eyes are closed. I try to open them to see her. I know she's here from her hand still resting on my shoulder.

"I'm sure she's just fine. Sleeping through it. Like you should be. Come on now, I'm going to give you just a little something to help."

I hear her opening packages. Tapping the syringe.
"It's a secret," I say.
"Okay now, shhh."

54.

The word "easy":

It's one of the first absences. No one tells me it's not a big deal. No one expects me to know how to make things work anymore. It comes as a shock. This acknowledgement of difficulty. It's antithetical to our normal ways. Our mask of indifference. Of ease. And so even though I wake up in the shock of it, I also wake up in this new arena of learning. This slower space. All these nets to catch my supposed fall. And the difficulty of trusting.

Even without mourning a loss, there is still a world to learn. I know I'm one of the lucky ones. It is more possible to learn without wanting to go back to yesterday. I had imagined myself in a shape somewhat resembling this shape. Had practiced slipping only one arm around Cat. Enjoyed minutes or moments of numbed out accuracy.

No one tells you it's easy to be a soldier either. Everything is louder and faster and there's always someone to tell you you're screwing up and weak and no good to anyone not even yourself. At least in the hospital things are quiet. Everyone tells you you're going to make it. That you've already made it. That you must be blessed. That they're here to help you and you're going to be great.

Things would be better without the echo. In those moments of return. The sudden resurfacing of knuckle. The clenching. The presence. This is what it means to be a phantom. Lingering in the afterworlds.

They show you how to button your shirt. How to butter a slice of bread. They tell you you're lucky or unlucky depending on the side you favor. I write out the names. Shaping them carefully across lined paper. Watching the letters sharpen and shake.

55.

Some of the memories I keep in reach:

This one comes over me in a solid wave. My wedding ring. I do not have my wedding ring. There is a second wave immediately following. That it has taken me this long to miss it. Everything goes hot. My pulse banging through my throat. Cat must have noticed. Cat must have noticed that I haven't noticed. That's the part that makes me sweat.

I'm meant to be learning how to shave again. How to taut my cheek single-handed. They don't give me a razor. They don't give me shaving cream or an electric shaver. Just a mirror and a red and blue toy razor. The physical therapist props me up in bed and shows me the motions. Moves her jaw to the side. Juts out her chin. Asks me to do the same. So there I am, like a five-year-old kid parroting his dad. And it hits me that it's gone.

"My wedding ring," I say. "I don't have my wedding ring."

"I'm sorry?" she asks.

"My wedding ring," and I hold up what would be my left arm. She looks at the space.

"Oh. Otis, I don't know." She puts her hand on my right shoulder. "We can ask someone."

She looks around as if the right person might appear. We're the only ones in the room. I don't realize I'm crying until I feel my chest getting wet. And then I realize I'm crying a lot and loudly.

"I didn't know. I didn't think about it." Choking the words. "I want it back. I want it back."

She's tearing up too now, standing up. Her hand back on my shoulder.

"I'm going to ask someone," she says. "Just stay here." And then a look of apology, of knowing that I am not going anywhere.

When the door closes behind her I hear myself get louder. Moaning. Mourning. I didn't know I could do this. I didn't know I needed to. I didn't know what I'd lost. I think about calling Cat. I want to tell her I'm sorry. I want to tell her I know. I don't know what to say about it taking this long. I should have noticed. I should have noticed the first time she held my hand. And here we are, one month in and only now holding the absence.

I pick up the phone. Hold it for a long time before I dial. I keep expecting the therapist to walk back in. But I'm alone now. No one is coming. There is all of this space around me. Closing in.

I press the last number and listen to it ring. I don't know if I'm hoping for her to pick up. I know I want to hear her voice. I don't know what I'm going to say. How I'm going to make up for this.

"Hello?"

I gulpsob into the phone. It isn't a sound I've heard before.

"Hello?"

"It's me," I try. But the words don't sound like words.

I hear her quick breath in, "Otis? What's wrong? What's going on?"

I've scared her. I want to take it back. I've scared her and I can't talk and I can't calm her down or make it better. I keep making these sounds I do not know.

"Otis. Is someone there with you? Put someone on the phone. Give me to someone else."

I try to find my breath. Try to find the exact center of my chest. Try to relax it. Somewhere inside this I am surprised that she has recognized my voice. Given that I can't. Given all these sounds that keep exploding. I quiet myself. Put the phone against my forehead. I can still hear her voice but not her words. She is telling me something. I have to come back.

I take five deep breaths. Bring the phone back to my ear. She's not saying anything. Just listening for me. Making sounds, "Shhh. Shhh."

"I'm sorry," I say.

"It's okay. What's wrong Otis? What's going on?"

"I lost my wedding ring."

Silence.

Long enough to make me say it again.

"I lost my wedding ring Cat."

"Otis."

And then nothing. Like my name is an answer.

"I was wearing my wedding ring. I lost my wedding ring. I'm sorry."

She's crying now. Softly. It's totally shitty to say, but it makes me feel a little better. Maybe that's community. I don't like that she's crying but now we're in the same place. Now we can find each other.

"I'm sorry," I say again. "I'm sorry."

"Shhh. Otis. It's okay." I hear the space between her words. I hear her deciding. "I have it."

I shake my head. Again. "I lost my wedding ring. I was wearing it."

"Otis, I have it. They gave it to me. I didn't tell you. I didn't know what to do with it."

Both of us breathing into the phone. Filling the space between us.

"They gave it to me in a plastic bag. The ring and your watch. They're in the bathroom. There's blood on the watch. It's not even broken."

Both of us are quiet now. I feel like I'm just waking up again. Like I'm just figuring out where I am.

"Do you want me to bring it in?"

I have to think about it. About someone taking the ring off my finger. The watch off my wrist.

"Just the ring," I say. "Next time you come. Just the ring."

56.

One moment laid upon the other:

After, she tells me there wasn't a moment before the phone rang. It was simply ringing. A constant state. Always there.

She says all the air went out of the room. She says she saw it push through the walls. White. Cold. The phone still in her hand as she got into the car.

She kept hearing sirens. Wondering if it was me. I tell her it couldn't have been. I was already here. She looks at me, shakes her head in two precise movements. Right-Left. "Every time I hear a siren I see you in the ambulance. I see medics leaning over you. Telling you to hang on. Pushing on your chest."

She tells me about the fluorescence. A man with square fingernails pointed her down the corridor to Emergency Waiting. Stenciled arrows on the floor. Blue on beige. There was a television showing a quiz program. Beige chairs lined up against the wall. She chose a chair facing away from the television. Put her fingers in her ears.

C081489T

I don't like the smell in here. The nurses look at me like I'm breaking rules I don't know about. Or like there's something I'm meant to be doing but nobody told me. I always feel like I'm in trouble and I don't know how to make it stop.

I hope they're not mean to you when nobody's looking. It makes me cry at night if I think about it. It makes me want to hide in your room just so I can check.

57.

The thin red line of before and after:

People think of a line as stable. Sometimes it is. It can set. But it doesn't start out that way. I guess it's the same way people think of staying still as stable. It's hard to stay exactly still. Not even a tremor. Not even the in and out of breath. We're meant to move. That's how bodies are built. Once you're still, completely still, that's the line you don't want. That's the line someone else will have to haul your body over.

You get to know the befores. They're hard to catch when they pass. But you get to know them later. You get to tell time by them. Life was one way. Then the thing. Then life is something else. It doesn't have to be better or worse. It doesn't even have to be big. But you get to see it over time. Bring it into focus.

There's the time before knowing her. The time before leaving. The time before coming home. And the time before this. There'll be more down the road. I can't see it all from here. I need a horizon. Something to line up against.

Before the accident I was not exactly waiting. Before the accident I was at a loss. I knew I was lucky. People told me and I knew it was true. But I also knew I wasn't right. I would go to groups at the VA. We'd sit in a circle and guys would talk about what they'd seen and what they knew. It wasn't like that for me. I don't know why I came home with a body and other guys got hurt. It's not easy to talk about in a room of broken men. Guys on crutches. In wheelchairs. Guys with compression bandages holding their skin together. They'd tell me I was lucky. And I'd say I guess I was. But that didn't help me understand.

Everyone struggles with return. We all have our ways. Invisible triggers. Usually in a room of twenty guys, there's only four or five who are working. And mostly they're still in. Some kind of desk job, but still in. Still able to serve. There's maybe another four or five with physical injuries keeping them busy. Keeping them working at being a body. And then the rest of us caught on the insides. Caught in some moment or series of moments. Playing over and over. Bringing us back. Keeping us from coming home.

I notice the patterns. Each one unique. There's a woman who repeats the last word of whoever speaks before her. Just a whisper. Just a start. There's an older guy who jerks his head to the left. Three staccato pulls then back to center. There's a flyer on the community board about PTSD. Little phone numbers to tear off and keep. I count the ones already gone and the ones remaining. Make a pattern I can stand.

I know it's Tuesday or Thursday if a volunteer helps me into a chair, wheels me down to a meeting. I go five weeks without speaking. Everyone looks to the bandages. As if harm is visible. Even though we're all the same. Night sweats and sudden fists. Words we cannot keep from shouting.

When I told the counselor I didn't need the arm, she said *It's not uncommon. Survivor's guilt.* But I always meant to survive. Always took it as a given. I told her that. I told her I didn't feel bad about coming home. I was just confused by mirrors. I didn't fit inside my frame.

The counselor told me *It's not uncommon. Post-traumatic stress disorder*, she called it. Who didn't wake up to sirens or lights? Who didn't break a shoelace and think it was an omen? It fucks you up. It fucks you up more in the after than the before.

I see it in the other guys too. Traces of repetition. Everyone's a different version. Everyone's a different scale. There's a guy at the Tuesday meetings who pulls at his hair. Plucks it out one strand at a time. Then lines the hair up on his leg. Tries to get the pieces parallel. There's a guy who can't stand the dirt. Says it reminds him of being there. Of never being able to get clean or stay clean. And so now his hands are raw pink. Broken skin. And he still can't stop scrubbing. Can't stop reminding himself he's home now. He's clean.

People talk about the drones. About a guy sitting in Kansas blowing up a warehouse in Kabul. I don't know if it's right, but it might be better. He probably still wakes up nights seeing faces he's never seen. But it's better than knowing. He doesn't have to worry that the guy at the next cubicle is about to blow sky high. He doesn't have to worry if his feet have been wet too long or if the line will be down when he tries to call home. He can get up and make espresso. He can go use the bathroom. He might have just killed ten civilians. But he doesn't have to know. He doesn't have to see their torn faces and he doesn't have to know.

58.

The lines close over and so do we:

Somewhere in the stages is acceptance. I was there before it happened but that doesn't mean I get to stay. Wanting something and not quite knowing. Days go by unconscious and I wake up almost as I pictured but not.

I never pictured the glass in my eyebrow. The gravel embedded in my cheek. My left collarbone a collage of hardware. I never pictured someone else's blood keeping me alive. This machinery of air and pulses.

They draw me a portrait of what they know. Broad strokes. I was here. This happened. This was the consequence. The whys don't matter. Or the hows. They ask me anyway. Everyone prefers a bordered image. It doesn't all appear at once. Some of the details are right there. Assumed knowledge. Others hide themselves. Impossible stowaways. I wait them out.

I don't know the whys or hows. I know where I was and I know I'm going to be okay. I try to show them how I fit together. How I'm almost exact. They say it's the shock talking. Maybe the medicine. They say I should sleep some more. We can talk about it later.

59.

On the confusion of instruments:

The doctor tells me we're going to try something new. She tells me it helps if you can see it. I haven't told her that I'm comfortable with disappearance. So I go along.

There is an open wooden box on the table. Split down the middle with a mirror. Two arm-sized holes on either side. She tells me to put my right hand in one of the holes. The rest of me in the other. I'm careful with the motion. Trying not to touch anything. Trying not to feel anything.

She tells me to look over the top of the box. To watch my right hand. To watch its reflection. I look up at her. I know this is a bad idea. She nods. Smiles. Tells me to try it.

I look down and I see it back where it shouldn't be. My arm. My hand. The skin healed over. I taste bile and my head turns in for a moment.

I look like any other person now. Like I never went to war. Like I never suffered. Like I don't know who I am. All my breath goes out of me. I can't even find the names. Pins of light. Funneling in.

"It's a mirror box," she says. She sounds further away than she can be. "It helps with phantom pain. Try stretching out the fingers on your right hand. See if you can feel it on the left."

I'm trying to stay in the room. Trying to keep myself from falling.

"We'll practice with the box when you get your prosthetic too."

"I'm not doing that," though I don't know if I say this aloud. I don't think I move my mouth. I feel sweat soak through the back of my shirt. The scar on my cheek is throbbing.

"Just flex your fingers."

And to make things quiet, I do. And it moves. And I feel it back where it shouldn't be. And then I am on the floor. The box on the floor. And she is picking things up. Checking my bandages.

"That's okay Otis. Are you okay? It can be strange the first time," I see her look towards the door. Worrying the consequences.

I look down at us. My arm is gone again. Everything is back in its place. I see our reflection in the window. Me on the floor. My shoulder pounding. The air too quick to grasp. Her hovering over. The window cuts us off at her right shoulder. I look up at her where she still exists. I look back at the window. Gone again.

60.

Seeing is believing:

When one object replaces another. When one object is removed or otherwise lost. We say that memory is kind. Meaning revision. Meaning *look away.* It is not possible to know a moment. To know each angle it presents. This is true. *And this.* This is believed. *And this.*

I arrange cones and rods and limbs to see an absence. To capture photons. I study laws of reflection. I polish surfaces. Maximize the specular. Recreate the shine of new grown skin. Watch while I pass by the silver teapot. How I seem so much smaller than human. How I am contained in this impossible space. These tiny parts of me. Combined.

Archimedes sank ships with less than this. Drove away a foreign army. Alice walked right through. As if to thumb her perfect nose at Narcissus.

And I catch ghosts. Light-prints.

61.

The cold creeps up like a tide:

Dis)appearance is a temperature. I didn't know this before it happened. In the fantasy the gap was a continuum. There was a body. Then the body stopped. The world continued. I don't know if that's accurate. I can feel the difference now. Separate the seeing from the felt.

There was something symmetrical about it at first. The cool stream of saline moving through my right arm. The absence of matter that made up my left. Being no longer a thing. Being only this memory of skin and tissue. Of predisposed anatomy. Everything cooler than it should be. Cooler than it was in the moment before.

It is the way with extremities. Sometimes the blood can't make it through. Sometimes it slows. Or stops. Refuses the passage from heart to toe. All of these miles. All of this constant motion. It's a lot to ask of a body. A lot to take for granted. I wonder if it can happen with torsos. If it's possible to get a chill in the right shoulder blade. In the sacrum. I haven't heard about it but I haven't asked. People don't always offer information. Sometimes you have to go digging. Sometimes you have to make the words.

What I can't get used to is the specificity. That from shoulder to elbow I exist in a certain way. That I am contained. That this has always been true. That before the accident it was different but still true. Maybe different and more true. And now there's a kind of gap. Or maybe two gaps. The one that was already there. And this new inaccuracy. This existence I am trying to call my own.

62.

There shouldn't be a temperature or a differential:

A chill on the back of your neck. An inexplicable flush of the ears. It's not possible to be precise, but I estimate the difference at seven degrees. It's most noticeable at the fingertips. Most separate. Warming as it reaches back into me. Absence warmed by presence. Transmitted heat.

It's more common to talk about the knowledge of a thing. The existence. Next is the pain. Often a clenching. A constant and unstoppable pressure. Except, they say, if you can see it sometimes it does stop. And so we step inside these tiny boxes. Make a magic trick. Wave a wand. Watch it reappear.

There's something solid in the absence. In the unintended returns. I am almost myself and then it's back again. I wake up with a body I do not know.

They teach me to use the box for reappearance. And I go along. Practicing each day. But I do not tell them what comes next. That if I can see it I can disappear it. Reinforce my borders. Burrow in.

I ask for a glove. Thinking I can warm myself. Or that part of myself that is no longer myself. I watch it. Try to move in such a way as to appear to rub my hands together. But I can't find the angles. The exact motions. It seems to separate me more.

I place a votive candle at the end of the box. Fire to heat the outside in. I wave my fingers. Watch them pink. Only the right side warms. I wait some minutes for the left to catch. But all I achieve is a more certain distance. Which also begins to feel like weight. As my right hand grows tropical, that which I call my left hand grows heavier.

Less regularly, but often enough to note, there is a kind of chill that creeps up from the wrist. I can feel the absent hairs prickle. I try to track it. The external and internal surrounds. Perhaps it's something in the absent world. A crossing of the disappeareds.

This isn't what I wanted. This halfstate. This incomplete severance. When I imagined myself somewhat like this everything fit so perfectly into skin. I ended where I ended. No confusion. No hide and seek. This has been a disappointment. It is the way with fantasies.

63.

Paint by numbers:

There are symmetries to limbs and organs. A body can almost be split. A heart over here. A liver over there. An uneventful appendix. There is information kept to the left or the right. A preference for holding a pen. Tying a shoelace. We build for this. For a person walking up the stairs. Moving their right hand across a page. One foot on the gas and one on the clutch.

And so when one is stilled. Expectedly or unexpectedly. There is a responsibility that moves beyond the norm. An opening of pathways. A relocation.

This is an anatomy of the imagination. The myth of the normal. How a body might function in a perfect world.

Division can happen at any moment. Over days or centuries. A c/leaving of one land to two. On August 15, 1947, midnight drew a bloodline through British India. Ceremonies took place over two days. The Dominion of Pakistan on August 14. The Union of India on the 15th. All so a man could travel between. All for the sake of arrival.

We divide along longitudes and latitudes. North and south. East and west. The sun still rises where it rises. Even if we turn it to a question. The answer sticks. As permanent as blood on dirt.

64.

Because it was not mine and hadn't been:

In that last shot. Mine and not mine. When my body should have disappeared.

In the lingering I became a stranger. Interrupting myself. Placing myself in door frames. Camera obscura. Making it true. Making a temporary world to fit my shape.

We do not know our borders. Most people cannot mark their height on a wall. Try picking a pair of shoes by sight or by holding them in your hands. Try finding the perfect pants without slipping inside. We do not know our reach. The breadth of bodies.

That I am closer to accurate does not mean that I know myself. I lose myself to expectation. What I was. What I was before. And now. And after that. We are always movement. We cannot stop ourselves. Even the mirror confuses. If it curves in some unexpected way or catches you otherwise unaware. We become more or less what we are. Familiar and not. Strange and stranger.

The first time I lost myself without intention. There was only me and only bodies. It was a question of waking unexpected. Finding myself whole and also missing. We fit ourselves to ourselves. More than memory. Less than want. All the time believing we can choose.

After the first, the second. A new set of cells. Making myself recognizable. I was aware of inaccuracy but not of specifics. It was an ongoing condition. A kind of malaise.

Which is to say that I was nowhere. That I could not find my map. And I could not find my way. The directions were unmarked. The compass unreadable. There was no scale. No key. No crumb to lay upon the road. None of it belonged to me. None of it could fit inside my eyes. I've never said this in so many moments. The instance of disappearance. Memory of what might still come.

Once I saw a limb that was not my limb. It was shorter than anything I ever imagined lost. It did not feel like me. But there it was. Mine and not mine. Not the loss I desired or the accuracy received. I was caught in the mirror of it. And then I moved away.

65.

There are mirrors everywhere:

Not that they can catch the slippage. We still see what we see. Like a film laid over eyes or skin. It happens with objects too. How some people grow to need a thing more than they should. How they inspect their cars for the smallest scratch. How they see a yellow patch on the roof that no one else can see. I know about limbs and faces. Torsos and teeth.

In the sixth grade one of my friends went over the top of his bike. I found his tooth on the road and scooped it up with asphalt and pebbles and blood. I'd never seen anything like it. There were pieces of him still attached. I was only ten. I didn't know much about bodies. A tooth wasn't so weird. Teeth come out when you're ten. But that was my first time with so much blood. And my first time seeing the insides come out. His tooth had cut through his lip when he hit the ground. So there was blood from the tooth and blood from the lip and it was a lot. And when we got back home there was his face full of blood and my fist wrapped around the tooth.

It must have looked like I clocked him. That's what they thought when we first came in the door. Shouting at me about fighting and fussing over his face. He wasn't talking. I guess it was shock or something but at the time I remember thinking he should speak up, tell them I didn't do anything. I opened up my hand and showed them the tooth. I remember his mother prying his mouth open. It was the front right tooth. And she looked at it and looked at my hand and then we were at the hospital.

I guess they cleaned it up and put it back in. The doctor told me I did good picking it up. It didn't occur to me that you'd leave a part of someone's body on the road. That you'd run away from it. But he said a lot of kids wouldn't have looked. Or wouldn't have wanted to touch it. He made me feel proud.

The tooth was kind of grey after that. Like a constant bruise. But you never saw a kid smile bigger in a photograph. He couldn't see it. It's like every mirror he ever passed would just patch it over. He had a scar that ran right through his lip too. It didn't seem to bother him any more than the tooth.

People see what they see. I don't know what made him look past that tooth. What makes other people see themselves as taller or shorter or smarter than they are. What makes them think that everyone must be looking at how their ears stick out or how their left eye doesn't open as wide as the right. The eye flips an image and the mirror flips it back. Maybe it's something to do with that. The translation. And what gets left in the betweens.

They tell me not to watch the endings. To let the image rest on the retina. To remember myself. This perfect anatomy. Textbook case. I tear the pages. Fold them over. Make them as accurate as I can make.

66.

Parts of this will have to disappear:

Maybe worlds work like this. Premonitions of want. All of the things that make us. Piece by piece. Genetic construction. The consequence of being handed over to care. To some sequence of events. Some lack. Or excess. So many years go by before we know. Before we are capable of movement or speech. So many hands move over us. Some more carefully than others. So many possible actions. So many moments.

Maybe the borders are open to debate. Mutable. Permeable. Maybe skin is built to break. To close. This most self-soothing organ. This patchwork quilt. We wrap ourselves in maps. Whole territories of terra incognita. This country is twelve years old falling down the stairs. Here is an ocean of blood tests. Precise incisions. Parallel. Traveling down the spine and up again. This country here, behind the shoulder blade, I do not know. Something happened here. A transgression. A violence. Something passed through the skin. A foreign body. (Un)seen.

Maybe telling doesn't matter. The narrations of each part of us. Of how we got to be exactly here. Exactly this. Maybe the moment passes with the words. Maybe we are wasting our time. Maybe we should stop. Maybe we are trying. Maybe we will not find our way.

Maybe we are unreliable. Maybe the staircase was not a staircase. Maybe the legs that gave way were not our legs. Stories give way to stories. We do what we can. What we have to.

Maybe the rules can be abandoned. We know the shape a body is meant to take. The limbs and extensions. The internal organization. How the kidney is meant to function. The parts we can lose and the ones we cannot do without. There is an expected rate of growth and acceptable variations. Methods to deal with anomalies. To make them fit.

Maybe we do not really live here. Maybe we understand tomorrow. We try to plant ourselves anyway. Try to make ourselves more capable of movement. Of becoming what we know we cannot help but be. Maybe the little one knows how to get up and walk itself across the brain. Maybe this is part of breathing. Part of blood moving through a body and sometimes out. Part of gravity and aging. The intersections of time.

Not permanent. Not unaccepted loss. Not mine. Not not mine. Not any one way of being or moving or marking one's place. This is what I mean to say. That I did not know this was coming. That the first loss did not predict the second. That possibly they are unrelated. That there is A and B and the sequence does not predicate the cause. That there is still an alphabet. That this makes us want to believe. To string the moments together. To ease the gaps between here and there. There is a picture of a mouse holding a hat high above his head. There is another picture with the hat pulled down below his ears. We make a movie of it. Smooth it out. Maybe it's possible to see in some other way.

Maybe we can do without knowing. Maybe answers are just words. Ineffectual hands on bodies that prefer not to be touched. Maybe the answer is there without us. How quickly we turn our heads. Tones we hear and tones that fall outside our range. How muscles form. How they fall away.

They ask me if I thought about dying.

"Yes."

They ask me if I thought about dying on purpose.

"Yes."

They ask me if I did this. If I made it true.

"Yes."

They do not ask me about choice. They ask me if I drove the car off the road but they do not ask me if I drove the car off the road on purpose. And so the answer falls between. True and not true. True and not not true. Missing.

67.

The shapes we make:

It is easier to see if you look at one small part. We know the whole differs. We know the features are particular. None of this is surprising. But if we take it down to the smallest possible unit. Maybe something internal. The differences magnify. It's just a matter of noticing. Of paying attention.

I remember Cat noticing my lines. She told me Afghanistan made me old. She counted the grey hairs. Traced her thumb across the wrinkles by my eyes. She told me she liked it. That it was evidence we were growing old together.

It makes as much sense as anything else. Once we see ourselves as skin. Once we remember that skin is an organ. I wonder about visibility. If it makes us unreliable. If it gives us a false confidence. Makes us prone to failure. To falling.

There's a patch the size of a fist. Starting next to my left eye. Running into my ear and across the cheekbone. The skin newer than any other part of me. Younger. Without memory. A knotted line running eye to ear. A tributary breaking off and dripping down to the chin.

And so we understand that one person has brown hair. We call it normal that a person can have blue eyes or green eyes. That height can vary. We make judgments. I'm not saying we operate with any kind of grace. Just that seeing it can help us understand. Can help us believe that we are real.

68.

There is always a moment before knowing:

Skin grows towards skin. So unlike a limb. It reaches. Grabs hold with keloid fists. As if to carve a line of demarcation. Something that might keep for centuries. A geopolitical border. An armistice. A ceasefire.

On May 4, 1493, Pope Alexander VI established a boundary to define the New World. In my youth I was unreliable. Attaching myself to a person or a group. And so this scattered state. The Spanish over here. The Portuguese over there. A general confusion of hemispheres such that I cannot tell my left from my right.

This scar is a memory of gravel under grass. Evidence of feet traveling too far from the ground. Mapping is a mutable practice. I know this. Like the back of my hand. An enclave. Redefined.

69.

Part of knowing this is that I cannot say:

Given the leaps. The desire to make this from that. I wanted. There was a possibility that passed me by and I knew that I missed it. I did not think to get it back. I did not desire pain. I know that it comes to a person. I know not to call its name. I did not desire to be the signifier or the signified. I was not exactly stuck but my head was turned.

More than any other thing I worry time. I make a map of every event. Every mark on a body. On a landscape. I try to mark the sequence. Allegro. Adagio. Repeat. There is a refrain I do not hear for years. I lean into a future memory. Try to catch it. Slip. Almost. Here.

Because this happens and that happens. Because we have come to rely on roads. On doors that allow for exit and entry. On possibly collisions. Permanent signage. One way streets.

Also there is this rupturing of bodies. Of light that escapes them. This is necessary. To stand exactly here. To allow this. To let this in.

Because of the mirrors. Because of the confusion of left and right. Bodies divide and we follow. Alien fractures. Sudden. Loss.

This is also true: I saw it before waking. Not every night or even most. But often. Significant enough to name. To label recurring. To hope for before I fell asleep.

And this: Had I known I would not have left the

house. I would have gone into the closet. Told her to trust me. Told her to wait.

And here we are. Told and foretold. And here we are. Making a nuisance of time. If only we could undo the hours. If only the words had not yet left our tongues.

70.

Closer and closer and then the wall:

A lot of this happens on the inside. I'm used to counting the breaths and pulses. And now I have this machinery. Measuring my blood pressure. My temperature. There are peaks and valleys for the heart. A tightening across my finger. My bicep. Recording my numbers. Watching them move beyond my grasp.

This takes all of my concentration. It's easier if the nurse is in the room. If she sees me watching she starts to explain, "That's your blood pressure. It looks like you just run low."

I nod as a way to shake my eyes to something new. To break it.

"It's in the range," she goes on, "Try not to worry about it." As if I could live inside a range. As if I could be so inexact.

I try to keep my eyes on Cat or my parents when they're here. As a way of not getting stuck. I guess it's still stuck but it keeps me in the conversation. Keeps me looking where it makes sense to look. It doesn't work if they sit too close to the monitors. My eyes stray. I pull them back. But not before they see. Not before they trace the path with me. Not before they notice what I notice. Each of them has only done it once. Or Cat's done it once and my dad did it once and must have told my mom about it. Now they sit further down the bed. In the open space.

When I'm alone I try to keep my eyes closed. At first I tried to make things move. To slow my pulse to get it to a multiple of five. To change my temperature. Stop and start my heart. Then I tried looking away. Keeping my eyes on the window sliver. Keeping my eyes on the television. But they always found their way home to the monitors. I think about asking someone to turn them the other way. So I can't see the readouts. But that would be telling. Better to do this my way. Better to keep things unconfused.

71.

Some of the threads that hold this together:

I learned to see letters that other people could not see. If a sign would fit perfectly with one more word. If a space was better filled than not. I could manage that by looking. Once you see a thing it's hard to subtract it. Everything lingers. A certain taste. An assumption of wholeness.

I research absence and presence. Trying to match them. To name the gap. There and not there. Visible and no longer mine. That the arm was attached to my shoulder. My torso. That my blood would pink its fingers. That my pulse could be seen at the tip of its thumb. None of it made it mine. None of it brought it closer to me. No matter how I held it. How I tried to work it in to every other part of me.

It started and I did not recognize that it had started. I did not know it was a way to be. How an arm can be there and be absent. No longer mine to move. No longer mine to hold. It was visible and visibly mine. But that was just a way of seeing. It didn't make it real.

When I was twelve years old there was a party that was meant to have a clown. The clown didn't come and we were sitting on the grass not knowing that there wasn't going to be a clown. And Bobby's dad shows up with this puppet. A marionette. Everyone's laughing. Everyone's looking at the puppet and watching how Bobby's dad isn't even trying not to make his mouth move. And I start watching the strings. How he pulls on this one string and the puppet's right arm and right leg go up in unison. Bobby's dad starts on about it. How the puppet's trying to put his hand up in class to answer a question and he keeps kicking the kid in front of him. Everyone's cracking up. I try to concentrate on the story. On this poor kid who keeps getting kicked by the puppet. Everyone's cracking up and I want to be cracking up with them. But I get stuck. I get stuck on the string between arm and leg. The string between Bobby's dad and arm and leg. How one thing is three things.

For a while I would wake up and feel the string between my arm and leg. I'd get tangled up in it. My dad would come in and turn on the lights and pull the blankets back and show me that everything was okay. That there was nothing tying me together. The puppet strings were clear fishing wire so it always seemed that they could creep in without you knowing. You had to look closely. You had to feel around. Just because you couldn't see it didn't mean it wasn't there. I feel like most kids know that. We're meant to grow out of it and mostly we do. But if that's how you see the world from the beginning, you can't let it go completely. We can't all get born wrong. With the wrong ideas. The wrong way of knowing the world. Some of what we know before we learn things has to be true. Like that first gasp in. The first time a shape becomes a face. The first time we find our feet. Our hands.

I was not one for imaginary friends. Relationships troubled me. It was enough to know the people I knew.

To navigate the necessary. I could not do more. I did not want to be the puppet master. I knew the tables could turn at any moment and it was hard enough to sit alone. I had friends. I was able to be in company. But each person needed to take charge of their own self. Each person needed to be visible.

I stayed away from games I couldn't see. I learned to turn my back. To move my gaze from the invisible to the unavailable. Just slightly left of my field of vision. Not not there. Not not known. Not not real. Unbidden. It was a question of positionality. A choice I learned to make myself safe. To keep myself in the room.

The first time my arm reappears it is a new thing. Far from a replica of what was. Three inches shorter and a half-inch smaller in diameter. Not withered. Just reduced. Reproportioned. It is not always there, but when it is there it is always the same. Slightly missing at the edges. Hovering. It moves exactly with me but I cannot move it. I cannot find the part of my brain that unclenches a fist. That disappears an itch. That understands that a fingertip is a dry place. That keeps the thermostat steady and bearable. That keeps the thermostat in relationship with the immediate environment. Which is the body. Which is the room.

72.

Learning how to be:

Other kids get stuck in other places. Sometimes it's a stutter. Sometimes a temper. A shyness around girls or strangers. There are kids who can't be in a crowd. Kids who can't sleep over. All of us, we have our things. Some are easier to navigate than others. We grow around them. Learn to make the room or make the changes.

My mother told me not to be embarrassed. That the fives were also about caring. About wanting something and knowing something. She said it wouldn't even matter except that it seemed to make things harder. Except it took up the room of caring about other things. That's why we were changing. Not because it wasn't right. Not because I was broken. Just because it might be easier to loose my grip.

My dad would nod and put his hand on my shoulder. He would help me with the games that Lanie taught us. He was good at following. He was good at keeping to the rules. He liked to have a template.

It worked for them and it worked for us. My mother would find the landscape. She would tell us what it looked like. Tell us how to live there. There were rules but there was room inside them. She would notice when things got out of place. But she would let them be. She would only tell us there was movement. Ask us if we were all okay. It sounds stricter than it was. It's good to have a boundary. Good to know your lines and how to change them.

I didn't know this until I was older. I didn't see them as two people until they moved away. When I was a kid it was me and them. I still saw them as one. Maybe it was meeting Cat that helped me separate. Maybe I was seeing what she saw.

My dad has always been the quiet one. My mother talks to fill the space. To build the landscape. She talks to understand. To calm herself. To keep things going. My dad listens. Learns the details. How to move around them. How it feels from every angle. Where he likes to sit. The best entries and exits. He learns who else is in the room. How to share the space. How to know when the pause is long enough. When it's time to speak and how to stop again.

I've never been good at picking who to talk to. Cat explained it when we were planning the wedding. The daily details went to my mother. The small things. The fabrics and menus. The font, the flowers, the napkin rings. Even when we didn't care about it, we could talk to her and she could care and it would make her happy. It would turn the planning into a gift. Into something she could give us. And she could bring my father in. Paint the landscape. Tell him why it mattered. Tell him what it took to make it work. The things we did care about, the things we needed to keep from question, they went to my father. It didn't matter if they went as a question or a statement. If it was a question, there was always room to change the answer or to give the answer alongside. And then the landscape was already there and by the time it got to my mother, it was a solid. It was something we could lean on.

Cat told me she tried to call my father after the accident. That she wanted him to tell my mother. That she thought he could be calmer. That she wished I had a brother or sister. That she would have told them and asked them to go to my parents' house. That if they lived closer she might have left the hospital and gone herself. She left two messages on his cell phone. She didn't want to call the house because my mother nearly always answered the phone at the house. She planned it out before she called. She was going to say, *Everything's okay. But Otis has been in an accident. He's in the hospital, I'm here with him. It was a bad accident but he's going to be okay. He's not awake yet. I think you should come so that you're here when he wakes up.*

She told herself she'd try the house if he didn't pick up the cell this time. But he picked up. And then she started crying.

"Cat?"

She knew the words and she tried to say them. She tried to make the sounds of *Everything's okay* but everything wasn't okay and she was crying and it was the first time she cried.

"Cat? What's going on Cat?"

She was heaving, gasping. She was trying to catch her breath.

"Cat, I need you to calm down. Where's Otis? Is Otis there with you?"

She took a breath and held it. Counted to ten.

“He’s an accident.”

And she breathed out with the words and then she was crying again.

“Where are you Cat? Tell me where you are. Is Otis okay? Are you okay?”

“He was in an accident.” Breathing. “He’s going to be okay. Tell me he’s going to be okay.”

73.

Only the sky is big enough for numbers:

Only the sky is big enough for names. So even when I can't get to it, I get to it in my head. I place the clouds exactly where I need them. One less thing to navigate. One more thing to take in hand.

I note the new names of the hospital and file them in with my collection. The nurses and therapists. The doctors and volunteers. Some of the drugs could be people. Especially in another language.

With the clouds exactly so, I punctuate the names. I place one after each movement through the alphabet. When I was walking, the clouds were in control. I might still have six great J names and have to move on. It led to a certain inexactness. Or incompleteness. I used to wonder if I might have gotten there without the cloud cover. If the skies had been more open. It would work the other way too. I'd be all out of M's and not a cloud in sight. I'd try to move to the N's, but some part of me would stay behind. Wondering what the clouds were trying to tell me. If I wasn't meant to go quite yet. If there was more to know.

The exact spot in the sky was always changing and always steady. I wouldn't look at it but it was always in my sight. Which isn't to say it was peripheral. A cloud could move right next to it and it didn't matter. I didn't even have to think about it. I knew the patch that mattered. The one that triggered change. It was maybe the size of my outstretched thumbs and forefingers making a circle.

It's strange that the sky is more mine in its absence. I can see the smallest slit of it from the window. Mostly I see roofs and walls. But there's the smallest patch of sky. Too small to rely on. The clouds move through too quickly. I'm lucky to get three names per letter and I never get to five. I learn to turn away. To use what's inside me. Maybe the other space was bigger than thumbs and forefingers. It must have been more like an open circle. Like I was holding a beach ball.

It helps if I focus on a space. My eyes aren't exactly closed. There's a gaze they teach in the meditation class. Where you're kind of looking down your nose but not at anything in particular. It works better than eyes closed. It lets me make things up. Which I think is the opposite of what it's meant to do. I look down into nothing and I see the open blue and let the clouds pass when they pass and I go through my names.

It's easier when I'm alone. Which is the same as walking. I don't like to lose my place. Which happens in conversation. Or attempted conversation. I don't like to get interrupted by anything but clouds. There are always people in and out of the room. If I close my eyes sometimes they think I'm sleeping. They still do what they do but at least they don't talk to me. If it's not too long I can keep the sky going. Keep the clouds moving across. Even while they're checking the chart. Changing an IV. I just keep my eyes closed. Keep going through the names. Some of them probably know I'm faking but they let me do it anyway. Maybe it's easier for them too.

I think about how it will work later. It probably doesn't do much good, but there's a lot of time here. Time enough to go through the options. Imagine the scenarios. Whether the imagined sky will work on the outside. Whether I'll be able to do it when I'm actually walking instead of walking in my head. The imagined world is eyes down. The beach ball is up. It seems that might matter. I try the imagined world eyes up. I try it for three days and can't make it to five. It's distracting in a nonspecific way. I can make most things work, but not that. The imagined world is down. There's nothing I can do about it. I try shifting it up just a little each day. But there's a way of looking down the line of the nose that just works. I get what I get from it. All of the sky. The clouds. The numbers and the names. But I know that there's more. I know that there's also a calming that can come. With the not looking. I know I'm not doing it right. I'm not even trying.

There will be months of inside before I get out. And now I can walk without walking. That's something I can keep. Even when I'm back on my feet. All of those nights trying to let Cat sleep. I'll be able to pace them out. I'll have the night sky. Maybe that's what I need to find the names.

74.

There's this feeling of responsibility:

Like I wished it away. Like I couldn't fit it in the room. One left forearm too many. I knew I should have left it over there. But it came back with me and I didn't know what to do with it anymore.

Maybe I can call it premonition. Things don't happen in any regular kind of time there. Everything speeds up or slows down. The next breath feels out of reach. I knew things I shouldn't know. So maybe I knew this. I didn't make it happen. I just understood it would happen. I don't know if it matters. But it complicates me. I get stuck. And then I have to start again.

75.

There is a slippage of here and not here:

Objectively I know this. Maps change with time. Lines move or disappear. There is a crater where there was a mountain. Ocean where there was land. Names change more quickly than languages. That has always been true. We would speak about it if we had the words.

Before the accident I practiced making my arm disappear. I learned to sleep on it and not roll over. I had whole minutes of accuracy. It depended on stillness. Even turning my head or shifting my foot could break it. The return was painful. Like needles I couldn't get at. First scraping at me and then jammed all the way to the nerves. Everything shook and then it settled. The settle was stronger that the shake. The constancy of it. The insistence of being.

I learned how to do it in VA classes too. I was meant to be calming my mind. We would sit together quietly. They liked to start with a quote or something else that's meant to make you feel good. And then we just sat. They told us to concentrate on our breath. In. Out. And I just sent it there. If I stayed still. If I found my borders. Lined them up against the skin. I could sometimes get there. And if I could get there I could make it last longer than waking. I could separate. And I always separated at the exact same place. Like it wanted to leave. Like it was waiting for permission. The longest I kept it gone was forty-three minutes. I got good at it. And when it came back it came back. Not there and there. No needles. No warning. One time I almost fell over with the weight of it.

I still try. When I feel what isn't there. It's harder now. I wake up with my fist cramping and there's nothing to push into the mattress. I can't disappear the disappeared. One time I thought I could run it out. Like it was making up for lost time. Clocking the hours I'd subtracted. But we're past that now. Even accounting for hours when I might have been sleeping. We're a long time past that.

A lot of guys talk about it. A thereness that lingers. That spikes.

76.

There is no such thing as repetition:

We have our ways. Each of us peculiar. Each of us following a wax-paper pattern. There are things I do to keep it normal. Another person's definition. Another person's home.

I know that numbers are dangerous. I know that letters are also numbers. I do what I can to steer around. Given the landscape. The history.

I say the names with each imaginary step. Avoiding the count. Occupying the places that tempt me. I try not to think about the shapes. Just the pieces inside. Mostly I fail but it's what I have and what I do to keep from sinking.

There are other ways. I know this. There are more successful ways. I could have asked. Then. But I kept on walking. One name to the next. Past the numbers. The noise.

People walk in and out. They sit and stand. Pace the room. Check the window. Check the chart. Busy themselves with the details of who I am. Who I was before. And now.

I picture myself crossing the room. Out the door and down the hall. I hear the soft swish of swinging doors. Automated entries. Everything muffles. Someone says my name and I'm back. Immobile.

And so because I am three months in one room. And so because I cannot walk without aim. I lean into phrases. Turn them into numbers. Rearrange the parts to make it right.

I know how many times they say *Great Job* each day. Each hour. I know how to get one more out of them. I know how to make them stop. I modify the pain the nausea so that the doctor orders just the right amount of each drug. It takes weeks to get this right. I have nothing but time. I watch it divide. Replicate.

77.

Only insistence:

If the hand reaches for the five before I blink. If I wait eyes watering as long as it takes. If I don't break contact. If someone comes in. If they speak to me. If they pull the sheets down to check on some physical notion. If I'm strong enough. If I insist.

It's the then that disappears. The payoff.

Some people say it calms them down. It doesn't feel like calming. Nothing happens to my breathing. Or maybe there's one breath when I get there. Just enough for the uptake. Just enough to start again. Maybe that's it. The restart. The constant motion. Even here.

I watch the drops through the IV. Count the panels in the ceiling. Listen for the change in gait of each nurse. How many steps from desk to door. How many words to answer the phone. I count the items on the food tray. Count the sips in each glass of water. Regulate my words. My pauses. There is always the need to get to the next one. Knowing I should stop. Knowing it's getting worse. Getting harder.

I tell myself that if they let me out on a day divisible by five. I try holding the pill under my tongue for the count of five but it starts to chalk, to bitter. Every time I lose a bet I have to make five more. Every time I win I have to make another. All of this motion. All of this over and over. Here I go. Pause. Stop. Here I go again.

78.

This is a lesson about holding:

The physical therapist places the jar beneath her forearm. Presses it to her body. Shows me how to turn the lid. Screws it off and then on again. Passes the jar to me. Her left forearm never moves.

I wedge the jar between torso and bicep.

"Good," she says. "That's right. Maybe a little more upright."

I make the correction and she smiles. I'm doing okay today. I'm staying in the lines. I reach across to loosen the lid. The jar slips and I pull back in to hold it.

"Keep thinking about the left," she tells me. "It's as much about holding as opening."

There's something humiliating about the fact that I'm sweating. I wipe the jar off on my shirt. Wedge it back in place. I reach across and it slips out again. Now my breath is faster. It's too hot in here. The room is getting small.

I start the fives to calm things down. To get my body back. Five names to hold the jar in place. Five names to open the lid. Five names to close it. I'm still sweating but things are staying where they're meant to stay. *Ernesto. Esai. Esau. Esmerelda. Esta.* The lid is coming off and on. *Etienne. Etoile. Eyad. Ezekiel. Ezell.* I'm in a rhythm. I'm up to F.

"That's good Otis. Now let's practice it with the jar on a table."

I keep moving. *Fabia. Fadila. Fairley. Fairuza. Faith.*

"That's good," and she reaches to take the jar.

Faiza. Faizah. Fanny. Fantine. Farah.

Her hand is on the lid.

Farica. Farida. Fariishta. Fatima. Fatin.

She's taking the jar. I pull away and it falls to the floor. Bounces once. Breaks. There are too many pieces to count. I'll give each piece a name. If it's a multiple I can find it. I feel close. I feel like I can get it. And then I'm picking up the shards and she's trying to break in. Trying to make me lose my place. Her hands are on my shoulders and I knock them away. Knock her to the floor.

And there we are. Broken glass all around us.

I shouldn't have touched her. I didn't know I would.

I watch her trying to calm herself down. Trying to remember the procedure.

"Okay," she reaches down to steady herself. Pulls her hand back up. Looks at her thumb.

"This is okay Otis. This is part of grieving."

There are two drops of blood on the linoleum. She puts her thumb in her mouth. I reach my arm out to help her up. I try not to see her flinch.

79.

I know I need to make it stop:

I don't remember all the bits and pieces from when I was seven. I remember a room with lots of colors and lots of toys. I played games with a woman called Lanie. Mainly she made me lose which made me angry and sad. She told me she was helping me learn that it wasn't losing. She told me she was showing me more ways of having fun. But it wasn't fun for a long time. It wasn't even nice. It felt like teasing.

I liked that her name was Lanie. It fit all my rules and I liked to say it as much as I could. I wanted an e at the end of my name too and sometimes I would write it that way but mostly I used the stop. Sometimes I was allowed to pick the games but not always and I couldn't pick any game, it was mostly the games she already knew and already wanted to play. When I was really good, which meant losing and not being angry or sad or quiet, she would hug me and tell me she was going to tell my parents I was her superstar. I wanted her to always tell them that so I did my best to stay inside her rules.

Sometimes my parents would play with us too. Lanie would tell them the rules and I liked it when they made a mistake and she had to teach them the proper way. When they won a game I would tell them they were my superstars and that always made them smile, every time.

My favorite thing about Lanie was that she never told me I was bad. Even if I got stuck inside one of my numbers and couldn't come out for the whole day, she would smile and tell me she knew I was having a hard day and we would try again next time.

I got to like going there. Even though I knew it meant losing and not getting my numbers. Lanie made me feel good and so I didn't need the numbers to make me feel good all the time. The numbers still worked and I still liked them better than anything, but I also started to like it when I could lose and not get stuck. Sometimes I would practice by myself. That's when I became a real superstar. An everyday superstar. I could take as many steps as fit into my walking and I didn't have to skip or stretch to make it right. I could stand anywhere in a line without getting angry. I could tell people how old I was without forgetting or lying or being afraid.

At our last meeting, Lanie told me that I was such a superstar that we didn't have to see each other anymore. She told me to remember all the things we learned and that if I ever got confused or stuck inside the numbers I could tell my parents and they would help me. I didn't get confused or stuck much anymore, which Lanie already knew. Still, it made me feel weird and I didn't know what to say so I just said goodbye and I waited at the door for my parents. Lanie said we could play one more game, any game I wanted. I picked I-Spy and we played it and I won and that made me feel a little better.

I don't have a Lanie this time and I don't know if I'd be able to talk to one even if I did. I try the games. Making myself stop short or go long. Trying different ways of doing things. It makes me feel like crap but I tell myself

I'm a superstar. I keep it going. Keep remembering the possible.

The hardest part is catching myself in the act. Lanie always set it up as part of the game. It was about noticing what I was doing and then doing something else. This time around the noticing is all on me and it's out there in the world, not in a playroom with someone taking care of me and saying nice things to me and to my parents. And I don't believe myself like I believed Lanie when I call myself a superstar. A grown man shouldn't need this kind of thing. A grown man shouldn't be playing games to get himself through the day.

I know it's hard on my parents. To see me back here. My mom asked me if I needed help. If I needed to see someone or talk to her or to Dad. I told her I was working it out. She said maybe we stopped too soon. Maybe we should have kept at it. She's right in a way. It was always there in the background. But for more than twenty years I was a nonstop superstar. So good at faking it that I didn't even know it wasn't real.

80.

All of these firsts to mark and count:

Which would be something else if my number was one or two. None of us remember the first step. The first bath. The first mouthful of solid food. We keep the ones that come later. The first kiss. The first close call. The first time we get away with this or that.

The first time I almost died I was eleven years old. It was my friend Tony's birthday party. He lived in a huge house with a swimming pool and lots of trees. Everyone from my class was there. Dive bombing into the water. Eating ice cream. All the parents were there too. Sitting in the garden. Eating sandwiches. After the cake Tony opened all the presents. There was wrapping paper and tape blowing around. I remember thinking it might get in the pool. That they ought to be more careful. But I didn't say anything. I was trying to be normal.

One of the girls got him a slip and slide. It was the perfect present for a pool party. Tony's dad ran it across the lawn and up to the edge of the pool. They had bubbles so it got super slippery and all the air filled with tiny rainbows.

Tony had the first go. We all lined up along the sides. There was music playing and everyone clapped and shouted. He took a good run up and dove all the way to the edge. Everyone was laughing and cheering. He wanted to go again straight away. His dad said he should let his friends have a turn first. But a storm passed over

Tony's face and then he was running up again. This time he stayed on his feet. Skating all the way across and then jumping over the edge of the pool right at the end.

After that we all started taking turns. Some of the girls didn't slide well. They'd stop halfway down the slide and look kind of embarrassed. It wasn't easy to stand up once you were on it so they'd kind of edge their way forward on their knees. Or they'd try to stand up and fall back over again. Everyone was covered in grass and mud. The pool was getting cloudy as they dove in to clean themselves off.

I could see myself sliding before I took my turn. I'd take a five step head start. Run five more steps on the slide and then onto my belly all the way to the end. Everyone would cheer and I'd jump into the pool covered in soap.

And so when it was my turn, I took my first step. My right foot hit the slide and just kept going. I knew I was meant to take another step. Another four steps. But that was five and that was danger. I was sliding across faster than I expected. My left foot found the ground and I kept skidding. I was still standing. This wasn't how I pictured it. I needed to fall to my stomach or maybe my back. I needed to get onto the ground. But I was so far across now. The edge of the pool was right ahead of me. I looked at the concrete and pebbles and saw my head smashed against it. Saw myself falling at just the right moment. Just the right angle. My legs zigzagged beneath me. My skull crushed. There was grass mixed in with blood on the concrete. Blood swirling into the pool.

Kids screaming and trying to get out before it touched them. All of this happened inside. All of this was a silent movie. I remember everything going so quiet. No one was shouting Marco Polo anymore. There was no more music. I could hear the bubbles rising off the surface of the plastic slide. I could hear the water streaming out of the hose. I felt myself tilting forward. Exactly as I pictured it. My head perfectly positioned to catch the edge. I remember the surprise of it. Of knowing I was going to die. Of not knowing I was going to die this young. I wondered if my mom was watching. I felt bad for Tony. For ruining the party. For making a mess. I felt bad that they'd have to drain the pool to get all the blood out. And then I was falling backwards instead. My legs came out from under me and my feet slid off onto the concrete. Smearing grass across the grey. I was completely without breath. I tried to get up but everything was shaking. I crawled off the slide and onto the grass. Just in time for the kid behind me to dive bomb into the pool. Cheering as he hit the water.

I was still in my silent world. My too bright edge of here and not here. I could still see my head smashed against the concrete. Still see my blood swirling in the water. I wasn't a part of this anymore.

Tony's mom brought out more ice cream and everyone ran dripping and laughing to get some. I stayed where I was until I saw my mom watching me and then I got up. I went over with the other kids. Like I was normal. Like I was living. Tony's mom scooped the ice cream into cones and we all ran back to the pool. I couldn't get back in the bloody water. But I sat on the edge. Dangled my feet in. Watched the blood dilute.

81.

They tell me I'm ready and so I go:

They tell me I'm making progress and it's true. I know they're talking about the arm. They see what isn't there. I know they want to fill the space. I learn to tell them I'm not ready. To imply a future time.

The doctor goes over the possibilities. Surgical and non-surgical alterations. The average time and percentile of stump shrinkage. Acceptance rates and user patterns. Silicone and microprocessors. I let the words be words. I don't count them. I don't divide. It takes all of my concentration to stop from doing this. It gives the impression of listening. Of making choices. He seems especially excited about my nerves.

Cat comes in with more paperwork. All the details of discharge.

"We're just talking about some arms," he tells her. And she looks at me. Like she's trying to see inside.

She gathers up the books and medicine on the bedside table. Puts them in a bag on the end of the bed. I don't count the objects. I keep my eyes on the doctor. On the prize.

"So you'll be back on Tuesdays and Thursdays for rehab," he says. "The PT can help with the prosthetics. You'll try some on. Give them a test run."

I nod like it's possible. And he stands up. Shakes my hand. Shakes Cat's hand. Wishes us luck.

The nurse tells me I have to leave in a wheelchair. I

don't want to argue but I don't want to do it. I look at the watch pinned to her shirt. Exactly five o'clock. I know it shouldn't be but it is. I keep my eyes on the watch. Keep breathing. I don't want to say the wrong thing. I want to keep moving.

Cat tells her she'll take care of it. I get in the chair and Cat pushes me to the elevator. The bags are on my lap. We're almost home. The doors open and I wait for Cat to push me inside.

"Come on," she says.

I wait. Twist around to look at her.

She grins at me. Picks up the bags, "Get up, let's go."

And we leave the chair in the hallway.

C050302T

In the dream we were at the old house and there were flowers everywhere. There was music playing. I think it was cello. Which is weird.

I was wearing my wedding dress and you were in a hospital gown. You weren't sick though. In the dream you were healthy. Everyone was mad that you didn't get dressed. They thought you were making fun of me. I didn't mind though. I was so happy to see you. I was so happy you were there.

82.

There is only so much space to go around:

I never took up much room. Not as a kid. Not in the service. I always knew my place and pulled in from there. If everyone did that things might be different. But I can only do what I do. Other people need what they need. Take what they take. I'm not saying it's better my way. I know I'm particular. I know that's not going to change.

This time she told me about the house. I tried to prepare myself. Pull in a little more.

My parents and her parents and Cat and me. Everyone fits together somehow. We haven't done it except for the wedding. And that was dinners and planning. Not sharing a bathroom. Not whispers in another room. It would have been better if it was just the two of us. If she was the only one to see.

And so those first steps into the house. All this activity. My mother walking from the kitchen. Aproned. Catching me with damp hands. Passing me to my father. Telling Cat she should have called. Asking me if I want to lie down. A cup of tea. How am I feeling. I must be tired. I must be so happy to be home.

Then we are on the couch. Cat on my right. My father opposite me and to my left. Ready to step in. Catching my mother's signals. Her careful eyes. I do not hear the key in the door. Just the "Hello? Darling are you back?" Cat's hand on my knee as she pushes up and out of the room. My mother telling me how hard they've been working to get things ready. How busy Cat has been. How wonderful her parents are. How wonderful to spend some time together.

Cat's parents tell me I look well. They tell me they're sorry they didn't come sooner. Before the accident. That they wanted to, of course. That they should have found the time. Her mother hugs my right side. Her father shakes my hand. Someone tells me I need to take it slowly. Someone tells me they're all here to help. Whatever I need. They know I can do it.

My father brings in two chairs from the dining room. Cat sits me back down on the couch, starts a story about one of the doctors.

I look around the room. Stand, uneven, "I'm just going to go to the bathroom."

My father stands too. Asks if I need any help. Cat looks down at the carpet. Smoothes a cushion.

"I'm okay," I say. "I'll be right back."

I stand in front of the medicine cabinet. Watching myself get smaller. That I could need five people. That I could need that much. And then I breathe into the number. Each of them alone is a crowd. But together. Only Cat can fill a house like this. Perfectly proportioned. Perfectly spaced. I wouldn't put it past her.

83.

Not knowing the room and how I fit inside:

I wake up and the bed is all around me. The ceiling is further away than I remember. There is a different kind of air here. A lack of mechanics. I have grown used to the crowding of instruments. I close my eyes again. Remember I am home now. This is where I live.

From the light through the curtains I can see that it's already well into morning. I never slept this late in the hospital. There were always things to check on. Trolleys coming down the hall. It is so quiet in this room. When I turn around to check the time I hear my hair move across the pillow.

Cat's side of the bed is already made. It looks like division. The place where she sleeps and the place where I sleep. I smooth over the sheets on my side. Place the pillows across the bed. Make it look like one instead of two.

I walk to the dresser. Showering seems ambitious. I get out a pair of sweat pants and an old shirt. I go through the steps they taught me. Set everything up. Pants are easy. I sit back down on the bed. Pull the right leg on, then the left. Stand up into them. My feet are cold but I'm not awake enough for socks. I thread my left arm through the shirt sleeve. Stop to rest. To breathe. I try not to picture myself. Halfway dressed and a full day's effort. I reach behind me with my right arm. Catch the edge of the shirt. Pull it around and over. Thread my right arm through. I button four buttons. The top one comes off in my hand. I walk back to the dresser. Put it in the top drawer.

I see myself in the dresser mirror. I take a half-step to the left. There. If I end there. It's almost like before but there are bandages. I close my eyes. Open them. I'm so close. So almost me.

I walk back over to the bed. Sit. I think about getting back under the covers but now I can hear them talking in the kitchen. I smell the coffee. I should be out there. I should be normal.

I put my right hand on my right knee. Stand up. Walk out of the bedroom and into my family.

They're sitting around the kitchen table. It's too small for five, but Cat's at the stove. Making coffee.

"I would of done that," I tell her. Kissing the top of her head. "I must have slept in."

"You need your rest," my father says.

"Did you sleep okay?" my mother.

"It must be nice to be back in your bed," hers.

"I never can sleep well in those hospital beds. They never smell right. And they're always waking you up for this and that," her father.

"Do you want coffee?" Cat looks up at me.

"No." Five breaths. I know I shouldn't but I can't help it. "I think I'll do my exercises," I turn back to the bedroom. Everyone is quiet now. I walk away.

I close the bedroom door behind me. Sit back down

on the bed. I can hear them talking again. I hear the word *pushy.* I hear the word *time.* The sound of furniture across carpet.

84.

It's hard to empty out the words:

It mattered to all of them but it only had to make sense to me and to Cat. We were steady on the outside. Which I think was somewhat of a surprise to our parents. Given what they knew of our beginnings. That we could find each other. That we could make a home.

I knew my parents would worry about me signing up. History was a perfect world for me. Making sense of past events. Drawing lines and worlds between. The same classroom. The same students moving through the years. I studied wars. I taught them. I moved my students through the causes, the battles, the treaties, the loss. I showed them how maps move like waves. Like tidal ranges. And so to leave that behind. To enter the present.

When I told them I was leaving for basic training in three weeks, there was silence.

"Are you there? Did you hear me?"

Then my mother, "Ned?"

They were both on the phone. I could picture them sitting in their living room. My dad with his head in his hands. My mother gesturing at him to speak.

"I don't know if this will be good for you Otis," she said.

"I'm not doing it to be good for me. I'm doing it because I have to do it. I'm doing it because it's good for you. For Cat."

"Don't do this Otis. Please don't do this."

"Dad?"

"Ned, tell him not to go," my mother was crying.

"It's going to be okay," I told them. "I have to do this. I want to see you before I go."

"Otis," my dad said, and then a long pause before he spoke again, "Is this already done?"

"Semester finishes next week. And I leave for basic two weeks after that. I thought maybe you could come out for a few days. The school's having a party for me next Thursday."

"What does Cat think?" my mother.

"She's okay. She understands. We have a lot to organize. They don't really give you a lot of time."

"Maybe we can help with some of that," my dad. "Just let us know when's best for you and we'll come."

I heard him whisper something but I couldn't hear the words. My mother sniffing. Something rustling.

"I know it doesn't make sense," I told her. "Just trust me. I'll see you soon."

And that was that. A four day visit. The first and last day full of tears. Cat pretending that her parents weren't angry. That they hadn't accused me of abandoning her. Instead she told stories about her great-uncle in the Korean War. Took the phone into the bedroom when her parents called.

We pretended things were good before we said goodbye. But I knew it was betrayal. Endangering the body they worked so hard to save.

85.

Everything in its place and then:

I know it's from trying to help. I feel it sometimes when she's in the closet. Wanting to do something. To interrupt. Even though I know she doesn't need me. That's the hardest thing. The circumference of trauma. How we navigate it. And so someone moves a table. Switches out a chair. And next thing you know it's all different. Or just different enough to make you notice.

Cat says it started the night she got back from the hospital. *Don't you think it would be better for Otis if*, someone would say. *Come look what we did in the kitchen. What are we going to do about the bathroom?* Each night she'd move things back. Tell them we'd figure it out as we went along. *Let's wait until he's home. I want things to be the same when he gets home.* The things we can control. The visible world.

And then everyone left and I was still in the hospital. The house was only hers again. Navigating phone calls and treatment charts. Recuperation. She would get things back to normal and there they were again. Another round of visits. Rearrangements. All this back and forth.

This is the only space we have. These common walls. Upholstered surfaces. We make our shapes in the furniture. We know ourselves from our imprint. There's a way you stop when someone puts the picture frame back even slightly to the left of where it should be. An unintended slip. But when a person picks up a lamp and moves it to the other side of the bed. When your toothbrush is on the wrong side of the sink. It foreigns the territory. Things become unreliable. Even if someone else might judge it better. Even if there's some objective way of looking at it. It's not yours anymore. It's not ours.

86.

And just like that she disappears:

The visible fade. In the room. I watch her walk past the conversation. Tighten her shoulders. Someone asks a question. Inconsequential. I watch her jaw clench. I know she will not stay for long. It's not the people or the question or any other particular thing. There is just a crowding she cannot move around.

Everyone is turned towards me and I cannot make them turn away. They move coffee tables. Rearrange appliances. Try to beat me to the impasse. They research devices for buttoning shirts. Tying laces.

Cat's father asks me again about a prosthesis. Tells me I should take my time. Tells me to keep an open mind. Her mother tells me it would make things easier for everyone. Shows me an article about a transplant. Another one about robotics.

My parents seem to understand the no. Enough to know that it's a solid state.

It has been raining for three days. A steady drizzle to keep us in the house. There are appointments to go to. They take turns driving me. Suggest stops at the bakery. The bookstore. I do my exercises. I stay in the bedroom. Build up the walls.

My parents take over the spare room. Cat's take over her office. Her work in small piles on the dining room table. I ask her if maybe her parents should stay in the basement. If it wouldn't be good to have her place. She tells me it's not for long. That she's used to it. I watch her watch the door. After so many months of being alone.

She's working on a new family. She tells us about it at dinner. A surprise for a fiftieth wedding anniversary. The children of immigrants. All they know are the names of the boats and the names of their grandparents. They think they know the names of villages but they could be wrong and it turns out they are. I know she loves this. The digging. The deadline. Unlocking the details piece by piece. She shows us her chart. The white space of terra incognita. She hopes to discover siblings and reasons. She knows there are cousins.

"This has to be a happy story," she says. "Fifty years. That's something."

Names repeat with generations. I collect them like coins. I watch her fill the space. Crowd the landscape. Each evening she tidies the piles. Moves them to the end of the table. Covers them with a cloth. We ask her how it's going. She tells us the births and deaths of the day. The marriages. The occasional divorce. And then she stops. Having found an invisible line. Having decided that it's someone else's turn. That the piles should remain covered. Out of the way.

It's that moment of retreat. That there and not there. All of our silences. All of this making room. I'm used to seeing her triggers. To knowing why she goes away and when she'll be back. Allowing for the space between. But here we are. All of us in one room. One house. And I see her move into the closet without ever leaving the table.

87.

I tell myself they cannot see and so:

I smooth the edges. Pretend to move past the places that occupy me. I gather my fives. Silently. *If nobody knows*, I tell myself. *If I'm careful*, and I am.

I catch my mother watching me chew my food. I imagine her counting. Even as she pretends to look away. Even after I swallow. As I keep moving my empty mouth. Six. Seven. Take a drink of water. On the next bite I try to chew without moving. Cat asks me if the food tastes all right. If I'd like something else. I shake my head. Chew four more times. Tell her it's good.

There are always whispers. I don't know if the whispers are about the counting or the accident. The accident isn't a secret so I tell myself it has to be the counting. Then I tell myself they don't know. That they're probably talking about the arm. Or maybe about something that has nothing to do with me. They have worlds outside this house. Things they've left behind to be here. They could be talking about someone I don't know. But they're probably talking about the arm. About the possibilities. About when I'll come around.

I tell myself stories. About what they can't see. I tell myself Cat knows and she's the only one who needs to know. I tell myself I'll figure out what to do once everyone's gone. Once it's just the two of us and I can do what I need to do and then I'll be able to make it stop.

Then we're driving to the supermarket and my dad

says something about it being the fifth green light in a row. And I turn on him, "Why are you telling me that? What are you talking about?"

He gets quiet and slow and says again, "It was the fifth green. That's all."

Nothing for eight blocks. I twist myself around to reach for the radio.

"Are you having problems with the fives?"

I push the on button. Turn back into my seat.

"Otis, only we noticed some things. It makes sense."

I stare out the window, "It's nothing to do with the accident."

We listen to a country song, a weather report.

"When did it start?"

Even though I didn't say it did.

88.

Returning to the space we could not see:

I enter a room thick with words. These words are medical. IV. ICU. Everything abbreviated. As with time. As with bodies. It's not that I always think I am the subject. But given the context. The vocabulary. I do not mean to make them uncomfortable. I walk through the kitchen as if to exit. To excuse. Her parents watch me. Pull me back with their eyes.

"It was strange, Otis, to be back there." Her bruised eyes. So much like Cat's. Swollen with lack of sleep. "The same waiting room. Twenty-three years."

I don't follow. And then I do.

"Cat doesn't talk about Tom much," I say. "I didn't put it together."

"We've been back to the hospital," he says. "But not to that ward."

In twelve years I never learned the name of the hospital. It didn't matter where he was. It mattered that he died. It mattered that all her life she had a brother and then one day she didn't.

"When Cat told us where you were I went cold. I don't know why. We've had friends in there. But I don't know. It seemed like Tom all over again. I kept picturing you burned. Even after she told us there wasn't a fire, I just kept seeing Tom." She stops. Looks at her husband, keeps going. "It was the same when Cat told us you joined the army. I knew you were going to die over there. I knew you were going to leave her."

I count to five eleven times before she speaks again.

"I'm sorry Otis."

"I didn't know," I say.

"We treated you badly Otis," her father.

"And you came back perfect. You said you would and you did," her mother.

I stay still and silent to make it true.

"We only let her in to see him once. I don't know if that was wrong," her mother.

I don't say anything. It isn't a question.

"She was so small. They told us before we even saw him that he wasn't going to make it. That we were only talking about days. You can't imagine what that does to a body, Otis. That kind of heat."

I hear myself swallow. I hear myself breathe.

"The doctors said he couldn't feel anything, but I don't know. It was five days out of seventeen years. He was a good kid."

We're all standing. Surrounded by chairs. This is the weight of grief. This inability to move through it. How it stops you on your feet. I try not to think about the fives. I try to stay inside the conversation.

"I saw it overseas," I say. "Just one guy. I didn't know him."

"We thought he was at a friend's place. Two days. We didn't even know. All the chaos with the fire. It was different then. Living in the mountains. And the phones down. He was a good boy. She never talks about him?"

"Sometimes she'll tell a story about him taking her

to school. Or if there's something in a movie that makes her think about him. Or a song. She doesn't talk about the fire. You know Cat. She's quiet about a lot of things."

And there's the line. The shared silences. I didn't mean to say it. I know they know about the closet. But I don't know if they still know. If they know it now. I cannot let them ask.

"I'm sorry," I say, "I have an appointment. I have to go."

They take a step back. Both of them.

"Of course," he says.

"Go, go," she says.

All of our eyes somewhere else. Remembering.

89.

It starts with an absence:

Small disappearances. Daily gaps. There was a space that was our space and then it wasn't. In all of that time I never had the walls to myself. Machinery and bodies. Other people breathing. The here and there of sharing time. But it was different for her. There were months of quiet. Months of open doors.

The first time I came home she made a rule about going to bed. After so much time awake. We both had to go to bed at the same time. I had to stay there until she fell asleep. We couldn't go there alone. Either one of us.

And then the accident. She didn't go home for three days. She slept on a chair in the hospital for another seven. Trying to stay out of the room that made it real. Where it was only her falling asleep or not falling asleep. All of those pillows. All of that silence.

And then everyone in and out of the house. Trying to make room. Trying not to notice.

I never even thought about a storm. I don't know what it's like to be so confined. A room in a room. Everyone outside. There was a closet in her parents' house. I don't know how my parents know. We never talked about it. Until they are there and it is storming and everyone knows it's still happening. There's a way you know things in theory and then there's the seeing. A disconnect we cannot cover over.

No one speaks when she comes out. But everyone

is watching. Her mother overbright. Pointing out the rainbows. Wanting to go for a walk. My parents watching for a cue. Finding none. Remembering an errand. An urgent need for apples. And for the first time since I came home it's just the two of us.

90.

We occupy our spaces and move around:

I wake up and she's sitting on the bed. The curtains are drawn but I can hear the daylight coming in. I can hear the others in the living room.

"What's up?" I ask. Rolling onto my side to look at her.

She puts her hand on my leg.

"Nothing. I just wanted to be alone."

She looks so sad. Her voice so small.

"Come lie down with me," I reach my arm out to her.

She lies down, presses her back into me. I reach my arm around her. Her heart is beating faster than it should be.

"What's wrong, Cat? What's going on?"

"I'm just tired. I just need to sleep."

She's trying not to cry. I try to get her to roll over, to face me. But she stays turned away. I know her eyes are open. I can feel her staring at the wall. I stroke her hair. Kiss the back of her head.

"What can I do? What do you need me to do?"

I feel all the air go out of her body. I feel her deciding. She turns around to face me. Looks at me with her red eyes, the bruises beneath darker now. I reach up to touch them. She stops my hand. Brings it down to rest beneath her cheek.

"Can it just be us?"

"What do you mean?"

"I mean, can it just be us?"

"You want everyone to go?"

She nods. Looking down at the pillow. She reaches out to touch my arm, my shoulder. Her fingers find the metal plate that was my clavicle. I am trying not to pull away.

"Did something happen?"

She shakes her head. Her tears fall onto my hand. She traces over my collarbone and across to my left shoulder. I feel a ripple of goosebumps rise as she gets closer to the absence.

"I just want things to go back to normal. I just want things to be you and me."

"Okay," I kiss her forehead. She closes her eyes. "Okay."

91.

There's a thing I have to do for every lie:

We tell a fiction every day. But my fictions cross my hands behind my back. Right thumb over left. We don't choose these things. Any more than we choose a weakened eye. A curved spine.

We're sitting at the table. Wine and lamb. Rosemary potatoes. I raise my glass, "Two weeks home tomorrow. Thank you for everything."

Clinking glass amidst the protests that it is nothing. That they're here as long as we need them. That I'm looking better every day.

And I feel both arms move behind me. And I feel my right thumb cross over the thumb that is not there. I almost turn to check. To see its return. It's not the first time I've felt the phantom. But it's the strongest. Removed from eyes. From visible negation.

I mean to be saying that I am feeling better. That what I need to do now is just keep going. To get into a routine. I mean to be saying that the doctor told me the routine was key. That it should just be me and Cat now. That it's my best chance for understanding the daily. For getting strong. I have it all planned out. Memorized.

I try to move my left thumb. To stretch it out. To fold it back. I feel it moving out from under the right. Crossing back over. I want to tell them I can do this. To see if they can see.

Cat's waiting. I watch her eyes move behind me.

Nervous about losing the moment. I smile at her. Thinking that she knows. That she can somehow see this new control. She tilts her head forward, *keep going*.

I don't know how to pull it back. How to reattention myself. My hands are folded behind my back. It wouldn't be right not to say. It wouldn't be complete.

"The doctor says I should get into a routine. Get into new habits. Figure out how to do things for myself."

"That's great, honey," my mother.

By now my left thumb is tucked back under. Ready to continue. If I can move it, I can find a way to make it disappear. I pull myself back to the conversation. Rubbing the no-longer-there callous on my index finger.

I don't know how to say the next bit. I look at Cat. She gives the smallest smile. The smallest nod. They smile. I smile, "So I think we have to do the next part on our own. Figure out the routine. Just me and Cat."

Everyone is silent. And then her father raises his glass again. I disconnect the living from the dead.

"To what comes next," he says.

"To what comes next," we say.

And that's the end of that.

92.

After the room clears:

Bodies linger. And voices. For the first few days we hold the open spaces. Imagined territories. Real as bone.

She doesn't move back into the office straight away. Her papers stay on the dining room table. Sheets and towels pile up in the laundry. We buy too many apples. Too many loaves of bread.

This is meant to be the normal. The getting back to things. And somehow the days pass us by. Almost watching. We do not talk about it. This stalled agenda. We let it trickle through. Curious.

I'm still not meant to walk alone so I go up and down the driveway. She makes me leave the door open. Sometimes I see her through a window. Pretending not to watch. Pretending to cross a room. Or look up from a document.

On Tuesday I come back inside and hear her tapping at her computer. The dining room table cleared of work. I walk to her door. "Back at it," I say.

She turns around. Smiles. "Back at it," she says. Turns back to the screen.

I head to the laundry. Put the sheets in to wash. This is how we make it to the next day. Tiny steps.

93.

On the failings of symmetry:

I am the last name on the page and she is beside me. There is a line between us. A blank space beneath. If this was a map for children we would be a new tree. Tom would be there. Her parents. There would be a page about the fire. A page about where we met and when. The map only captures official occasions. Marriage contracts. Birth and death certificates. Divorce. It does not speak to lingering illness. It does not speak to relocation. Separation. There are no reunions on the map. People come into each other's lives and then they leave. That's all we see on the surface. So she tends to the ground beneath. Builds the foundation. Waters the soil.

These are the years I was not here. This is my return. Both of us in one space. Here is a mark of the accident. A reabsenting from home. And here we are now. This moment.

94.

She tells me about the leaves and shoots:

Each new branch is a universe. She labels them carefully. Leaving room for other languages. Undiscovered lives. There are codes to hold the hidden places. Letters and numbers. Directional moves.

She likes the surprises. The ones the families don't know about. The known mysteries are usually sadder. A daughter with lines that don't connect. A hastened ending. Or none to note. Someone to find or someone to blame. That's the endgame. The answer to a question they can't quite form.

But when the question isn't a question. When it's pure discovery. Even if the story looks worse for the searching. There's an ethics that keeps her moving through the vines. Keeps her following the ghosts.

I'm standing in the door of her office. She's at the desk. Working on a map. I can tell there's something new. Something nobody knows or thinks to ask. I ask her if she ever keeps the secret and she looks up at me as if accused. "It's not my secret," she says. "It's their world."

I don't know we've moved into danger, so I keep going. "But if it's something you know will hurt? Do you think about it?"

She spins her chair around. One full rotation. "I tell them I've found something hard. Sometimes they ask me not to say more." Another turn. "I just don't like it when they ask me to keep something out of the documents.

It breaks the papers. I can always see the space. If they tell me not to say, I put it in an envelope. In case they change their mind. That way it's theirs. That way I'm not deciding for them."

She turns back to her desk and I stand there a moment longer. Watching her tracings. This person to that.

95.

Some of the things I have to learn again:

Like buttoning my pants. Tying my shoes. There are devices to make each thing possible. There are ways around. Avoiding the buttons and laces. Working through the absence. It is easier to be elastic. Easier to slip my feet inside. All of these things we take for granted.

There's a door knob that fits onto the steering wheel. A reconfigured column so that all of the buttons, the levers, operate on the right. They can install a latch to open the door without leaning across. I'm not there yet. Maybe another month or so. My shoulder needs to heal some more. I'm getting closer.

First I have to learn about liquids. Pouring hot water into a cup that might move at any moment. Cutting up my food. There has to be a way to do these things. I circle a dishcloth around the base of the cup. Steady it. Pour. Make a solution. I try to cut things with my fork. I avoid foods that make this difficult. Pretend an alteration in my tastes. I take to eating with my hand. But this is also more complicated now. I look for a solution inside the solution. Piecemeal the answer. Limp along.

There are things you don't even think about. Putting toothpaste on your toothbrush. Wetting it down. Turning the water off again. On again. We live in a two-handed world. That probably isn't true. We live in the familiar. And I grew up in a two-handed world. I'll always be a step behind someone who was born with one. Figuring out the systems. Stepping into patterns I can no longer hold.

There's a general slowing down. I can do one thing. I can stop doing that thing and do another thing. Move back to the first. Or on to a third. Simultaneity is no longer possible. All of these things happening at once. Merging. The juggling act of everyday tasks. Getting something out of the fridge. Locking the door behind me. Drinking a cup of coffee while reading, while typing, while doing any other thing that involves motion. I've never been a fast mover. I pride myself on being steady. But sometimes it starts to feel like I'm waiting. I get impatient for the basics. The daily moves.

I'm trying to get used to writing. Trying to find ways to steady the surface. To hold the pages in place. I find myself avoiding this too. Cat's always taken care of the bills. Of the grocery lists. But there's so much paperwork now. Hospital invoices. Insurance applications. I shuffle them into piles. Rearrange the order. I do every other thing before I touch pen to paper.

Telephones are also more trouble than they used to be. A conversation becomes a movement. Isolating all other possible actions. I try using speakerphone. But it makes for a different conversation. A different kind of listening and different words.

I'm scared of losing my balance. There's a lean to the right. An overcompensation. At first I try not to carry things. Thinking it would exacerbate the issue. Then I try carrying a bag in my right hand. To weigh me down. Keep me on the ground. The PT says it's not good for me. That I have to get used to being alone. Just me in the space. Without props. Without devices. Which seems ironic. Given my refusal of the recommended prop. The prescribed device. So I pretend that the bag has content but really it just has form. I experiment with weight. Just enough to keep me on my feet. To feel the movement from step to step. I pack and unpack the bag. Keeping the insides private. It's only old t-shirts and recycled paper. But nobody needs to know that. Nobody needs to see.

96.

I make a system and I make it work:

I know to be careful with repetition. Everything I learn is a division. There's the way you do things with two arms. Two hands. There's a different way with one. They teach me how to hold a bottle in the crook of my arm. How to break each movement into its components. How to separate the pieces. They tell me to do it the same way each time. To make a new habit. That's probably a better idea for other people than for me. I look for the subtle variations.

I put my left arm into the shirt first. It doesn't feel natural. I never did it that way before. It's still packed with bandages and tender to the touch. Even the slightest brush against fabric sends an ice shiver through my scapula. Sends bile to my throat. I have to sit down on the bed again until it passes. Until the spots disappear from my closed eyes. Still it's safer to thread the left one through first. Slowly. Carefully. First the absence and then what remains. Once it's through to the shoulder, I reach around with my right. Pull the shirt up over my shoulders. I try buttoning it from the top down. That's easier than working my way up. But I make sure I try them both. Alternate. I try going back to the right arm first, but I never make it all the way. They tell me not to try t-shirts for another few months. I try one anyway. It doesn't go well. I end up on the floor. The roof closing in on me. I stick with button up shirts after that. Short sleeve is better but some days I wear long sleeve. I am trying not to form habits. Trying not to be dependent.

Cat does most of the cooking but I'm in charge of coffee. There's a drip machine we use when people visit but when it's just us I use the stove top percolator. I hold the bottom half in my armpit and twist off the top. Put the faucet on, fill the bottom with water, put it back down on the counter. Then comes the filter and the coffee. The hard part is getting the top back on now that it's full. I try holding it again, but the water drips down my arm, a river of coffee grounds. I try pushing the percolator against something to keep it still while I twist the top on. But it's too much pain. Too much contact. I make a nest with a towel. Place the percolator in the center. I can't get it to hold still while I twist the top on. I pull it towards me, cup it against my chest. I bend down and try to steady it with my chin. There's something humiliating about it. It's just me in the room, but it's embarrassing. I start going through the kitchen drawers. I don't know what I'm looking for. There are implements I've never seen before. Pot holders. Whisks. I find one of those rubber grips Cat uses to open jars. I was always in charge of jars. I put one under the coffee pot. Put it back in its nest. Twist the top on. That works for today. That's a new system. I stop and look at it for a minute. If Cat was home I'd call her in to look too. I get the stove on, get the coffee on the stove. Sit down at the kitchen table and watch it boil. I already know I'm going to have to stick with this one. I'm going to have to make this one a habit. I can change out the grips and the nests. I can pretend some false variation. But I know this is probably how it has to be. I try not to break it into steps. If I break it into steps I'll break it into fives and that's where the trouble starts. This will be one of the new ways of doing things. It doesn't have to be a problem. It doesn't have to matter.

I drink my coffee and read the newspaper. The front page has three stories above the fold and five beneath. Two are about war, one is a train station hero, three are financial, one the weather, one true crime. I start with the crime and work my way up. I try to read all the words. I count the headlines but not the paragraphs. I count the people in each story but I don't add them up across the page. That's good for today. That's progress.

I finish the page and I finish the coffee. I pace them out to meet each other. I leave the paper on the table and put the cup in the dishwasher. I put the coffee pot back in the grip nest and try to screw off the top. Nothing. I pull it back in towards me and see stars when it touches something not yet healed. The back of my neck fills with sweat. I watch myself pick up the percolator. It isn't meant to be like this. I walk to the door. Put the pot down so I can open the door. Everything is meant to fit. I watch myself pick it back up and walk outside. I watch myself throw it against the concrete driveway. This was meant to make me me. I watch myself pick it back up. This was meant to be easier. Throw it back down again. Not easy but easier. I kick it against the garage door. Denting the door but not the pot. I leave it in the driveway. Go back in the house.

97.

There's the sound it makes and the sound it makes inside your body:

Pretty much the only ground to stand on is your own. It doesn't have to make sense to any other person. You can try to explain it. Sometimes it seems like it might help for someone else to know. But all you can do is bring them a little closer. They can't get all the way in. It isn't anybody's fault. It's just the way we're made. All these borders and all this skin.

I used to try to hide her from the thunder. When we first met. After she told me about the closet and being alone. I thought I could change it but I couldn't even recognize the sound. A truck would drive by and I'd go into action. Closing the curtains. Closing the doors. And she'd just look at me. I never told her what I was doing, but she'd say, *It isn't thunder.* And somehow I'd feel guilty.

She's always one rumble ahead of me. No matter how hard I try. No matter how carefully I study the sky. I only hear the false alarms. She's already gone before I get there.

There are triggers you learn to recognize but can't avoid. The sound of a car backfiring. News helicopters. The fourth of July. They warn us about those ones at the VA. They tell us it's normal to respond. It's what we've been trained for. That hitting the ground is part of what makes us good soldiers. Part of what keeps us alive.

A branch snapping underfoot. Three rapid knocks on

a door. I didn't know those ones until I knew them. It's the same response either way. A cold and instant sweat. Nausea the size of a fist punched right into the center of my solar plexus. And my feet stop dead where they are. Listening for what comes next.

I know from knowing that it's better to tell her about the sounds. I start with the ones I can explain. Ballistics and transport. I don't tell her about me. Just about what they tell me. How you can learn to recognize the response. How it can help to look around. To remember where you are. That the first twelve months are the loudest. That after that you start to get used to explosions that aren't explosions. To helicopters that are just looking for traffic.

She tells me about a friend of hers who was walking down the street with her brother. And all of a sudden they're on the ground. Him on top of her. His chest pressing her face into concrete. People were pulling him off and asking if she's okay and she could see in his eyes that he was somewhere else. And she could see in their eyes that they didn't get it. That all they saw was a guy throwing her on the ground. He wasn't talking. Just looking around like he didn't know where he was. Like he'd never seen his own hometown. And she tells everyone they're fine. Thank you. And she takes his arm and starts pulling him back towards the car but slowly so no one can see that she's pulling. And she still doesn't know what he heard but she figures it must have been a car. They don't talk about it. She gets a bruise the size of a peach on her left cheek. But they don't talk about it.

I tell her about the branch and she nods like it makes sense. "That's going to make things difficult when you start walking," she says.

It's the sound of a branch snapping on dirt or dry grass. I'm mainly on the sidewalk. I'm surprised she doesn't know this. I think about explaining but I'm embarrassed that she doesn't know. And I think she'll be embarrassed if I point it out.

"Yeah. It's not really like that. The walks will be okay."

She nods her head like it makes sense or it's a relief. "That's good," she says. "At least that's good."

I tell her about the knocking and she nods again. She doesn't say anything straight away. I feel bad about the walks. About her not getting it. We're just sitting there. Looking at our hands.

After another minute, "How did you even know about that one? Who does that?"

I have to think about it.

"There was a doctor at the hospital. Always three knocks and then he'd come in."

"I didn't think doctors knocked. I don't remember any of them knocking."

"Yeah. It was just this one. But he did it every time. I don't know what it makes me think but it makes everything go cold and I just stop."

"Maybe that'll be okay now. Who's going to come here and knock three times? People don't really do that do they?"

"I don't know. The mailman. Someone who needs to

use the phone. It's just strangers. You can't stop it. You can't tell anyone."

"Like the weather," she says.

And I know she gets it. That even though she doesn't know the sounds she knows the way they feel inside. That even though I'll always hear it a moment before her. Even though I need to hit the ground alone. Even though she can't stop it or understand it or make it better, maybe she can keep me company. Maybe she can sit against the door just in case I need her. Just to remind me that there's a door and that there's something on the other side.

98.

There's a different kind of dark there:

Sometimes you can see right through. To the next day. Or another hemisphere. Sometimes you can make a home inside it. Turn it into a vehicle. Travel to a safe place. You can do it with covers over your head. Eyes open to keep out the red. To keep from seeing the insides of things. You can do it when the moon moves behind the mountains. When the stars fail. When everything pulls down on top of you and the only choice is to start again. To end the day. To name it.

We meet at the closet. Not a physical act but an intersection. When the sky gets too bright. Too loud. When things start to fall. Or threaten. We lean against the door. Back to back. Or almost. Temporary patched to temporary. Making a new sky. A new set of borders. We each have our country. Big enough to house us. Dark enough to make us safe. We are the light masters. We shine the sun. Command the moon. Stretch the days or end them.

Something happens to the sound when the sky darkens. Things become more possible. More your own. Voices detach. The words still hold themselves together but the threads mingle. Conversations disentangle and redefine. Still themselves but broken open at the center. Cored.

In the beginning darkness would still me. Not knowing the edges of things. Where I might fall off. I made myself careful. Made myself small. It started as an experiment. My foot inched out. My head turned slightly to the left. No one could see. Even I could not be sure it was true.

She reminds me that we were children. We were not in control of our bodies or where we kept them. She reminds me that we were born to this. That we made it possible but could not make it right. Something happened in the thunder but she does not know its name. She has lived this many years without knowing and given the choice she will continue. Knowing would change the light. Which changes everything.

Sometimes the light makes it through. It doesn't always reach us at the same moment. It's unreliable. As we are. I used to understand the length of days. How they move between seasons. Stretching. Retracting. Making themselves new. Making themselves mathematical. I calculate the hours between us. Imagine strata of day and night. A circle within a circle. Enclosed.

99.

Each of us with our separate shelters:

The smallest and largest of spaces. We have our separate times and reasons, but it's where we go when it's just us. Just us alone.

"Don't you ever need a roof?" she asks. Looking up at me through sleep-messed hair.

I pull her closer to me and brush the hair off her face. I know what she means and I know she doesn't need me to answer.

"Don't you ever need a sky?" I ask.

And she twists around and smiles.

"I have a sky. And a roof. And walls."

"So do I, baby."

She props herself up on her pillow. Tucks her feet beneath my legs.

"Yeah. It's funny though."

It's the closest we've ever come to talking about the inside of the closet. I could ask her about it now. But I don't think she'd answer and I don't think it's what we're doing. We're just walking around the edges. Surveying the landscapes we occupy alone. Noting our various geographies.

"I guess everyone has their place."

"I guess."

"It's maybe better this way. If we had the same place we'd be tripping over each other."

"Yeah." Her face goes somewhere. Maybe to the closet.

"I didn't think about that." Her eyes move from my eyes to my arm. I feel the absence reach towards her. See her eyes follow the movement of my shoulder.

"Sometimes I think that I can feel it," she says. "If I just look at your shoulder and kind of blur my eyes. It's mainly when I'm sleepy."

"I feel it too," pulling her in with the arm that's there. "They say it's mainly in the first few months. That you have to get used to the absence."

"It'll be different when the bandages come off," she says. "Everything's so covered over now. It's like it's still temporary. Like it's still changing."

"I guess it still is for other people. It still would be if I was getting an arm."

It's only in that moment that I realize how strange it is that I've never asked her. Not for permission. But just to ask. How it feels. How it is for her.

"Do you wish that I'd got one? That I was getting one?"

She pulls away a little, turns her head so her hair falls back across her face.

"I should have asked you this already," I say. "We should have talked about it in the hospital."

"I don't know. No. I mean it's not about the arm." I listen to her breathing. "I thought you were dead Otis." More breathing. More silence. "I thought there was nothing. And then it was just an arm. It doesn't seem like so much. Not now."

"There's going to be a lot to get used to," I tell her. "For both of us."

"We're good at that," she pulls in close again. "We're good at getting back to normal."

She's quiet for so long I think she must have gone to sleep. Then, "It must have been hard in the hospital," she says. "It must have been hard to be without a sky all that time. Especially then."

I didn't know we were going here. I thought we were moving around the edges. But here we are. Here she is asking.

"There were a lot of numbers. They kept things calm."

We're quiet for a minute. I keep thinking she's going to ask a question. But she just watches me. Waits for what comes next.

"How is it when you're out in a storm? When you can't get home?"

A veil comes down behind her eyes. A step too far.

"We're talking about you, Otis."

"We're talking about us, Cat."

I see the veil solidify. Turn to a wall. She throws the covers back. Gets out of bed.

"There are always storms. I can't stay in the house just in case." She's pacing the room. Her eyes everywhere but on me. Taking in the door. The windows.

I try to keep my voice steady. Five breaths to calm us down.

"I know. But I mean how is it different when you're in and when you're out?"

"I don't even know what you mean, Otis. I'm just trying to understand about the hospital. I'm just saying that I know it must have been hard. That it must have made it harder with the numbers. That's all."

She sits down on the bed. Her hands are twisted in her lap. I pick them up. Lift them to my mouth.

"It was hard not to walk. It made the numbers worse." A retreat. "They were already pretty bad." Her hands relax in my hand. "I didn't tell you how bad but they were worse after the accident."

Her thumb on my mouth, "I know. It's worse when I'm out too. It's the difference between being safe and not safe."

"It's better when we're here. When it's us."

"Yeah. You and me and the roof and the sky."

C112896T

Sometimes I get mad at the questions. It feels like I'm mad at whoever's asking the questions, but I'm not. It's hard to remember the difference. You're the only one who ever saw that. I remember you teasing me about it. I remember it making me even madder until I started to cry and then you were sorry even though you were right.

I miss that. How we could fight and it wouldn't matter.

Do you miss it too?

100.

Because it's not the shape we're meant to take:

We approximate the known. Mirror the difference. Smooth out the particulars of who we are. We learn how to sit quietly in school. How to answer the basic questions. How to make a pleasantry. All the social norms of sharing space. We learn how to dress like other people. How to wait our turn. We learn the concepts of fair and not fair. How to disagree without violence. How to stand our ground.

Some of this happens in conversation. Some of it is mimicry. A role that isn't made for us but that we learn to play.

A broken mirror means seven years. There are consequences of splintering. Even if we say we don't believe.

Czechoslovakia was a land-locked country and still it dissolved. There was one country on December 31, 1992. Then everyone forked their tongues, sang a song. Everyone kissed and there were fireworks. And then it was a new year and two new countries and all the maps were wrong again.

Some people fear ladders. Black cats. The color green. Some people fear an open umbrella. A Shakespearian tragedy. A crack in the sidewalk. An itchy palm. An itchy ear. All of these chains. All of these triggers.

So we throw the rice. Search for the fourth leaf. Do or do not step on shadows. We tell ourselves we're taking care. Listen for the owls. Try to blow out the candles in a single breath. All of these silent agreements. All of this time.

101.

It's always a shock, even when you see it coming:

Even when the forecast is accurate. There are things that a body can and cannot hold. Some of them are temporary. Variable from day to day. Others linger. Whether or not we notice their arrival. They are simply there and everything is different for it.

I ask if she remembers the first time. I know it's outside the normal lines. Not forbidden. But dangerous. Enough to slow us down. Watch our footing.

I don't remember the first time. Things happen on a curve. But her thing is different from my thing. I don't want to assume a sameness. So I ask her if she's always been afraid of storms. Even though we've never called it fear. Even though I'm not sure that I should.

She shakes her head. As if to shake off the question. Something passes through her eyes. Her head tucks back. A momentary retraction. I shouldn't have asked. Which I knew before the asking. And then her shoulders drop and it seems that she might answer.

"I don't remember," she says. "Or I don't remember the time before. It's just where the storms happen. Just where I go."

A memory of speech passes through me. Of medicated moments.

"That makes sense," I say. Not that it does or doesn't. Not that it matters.

"I used to think maybe I'd live somewhere else when

I grew up. Somewhere without thunder. Did you ever think about it? That we could go somewhere that never storms?"

Did I speak about the closet? Who would I have told?

"I never thought about living somewhere else. Are there places without thunder? I mean, we could go."

She's already shaking her head, "No, I don't mean that. I don't want to go. I just mean it's weird that we haven't talked about it." Her head tilts to the left. "I don't even know if I could. If I could leave. I don't think I want to."

The question is somewhere behind us. We may not get back there. It probably wouldn't matter if we could.

I don't know if I noticed the counting first or if my parents did. You can't always see your patterns. Standing inside them. Looking out. I know there was a space between the noticing and the saying. It's all memory now. Funneled into years. That's how we organize. Smoothing out the lines. Connecting the dots. The edges wear away even as we try to shine them. Maybe it's erosion. A natural change in the landscape. No less real than what it was before. Only different now. And tomorrow.

102.

As if to prove the act in the action:

A wheelchair means you were there. A general nervousness outdoors. A refusal of tans and khakis. If sudden flashes make you nervous. Not being able to tolerate ceiling fans. Drinking three beers alone in the afternoon. Not leaving the house for seven days. Tucking in the corners of the sheets before you go to bed.

Bodies become suspended. Interpreted by circumstance or likelihood. I know that people see me and they see a story that isn't mine. Sometimes I go along with it. Just to keep the quiet.

I am sitting on a bench outside the supermarket, Cat is inside. I am counting to five-hundred. I'm on my second round. This guy comes over and thanks me for my service. I shake his hand.

"My brother's in Afghanistan. He was meant to be home already but they stopgapped him."

"That's tough," I say. "I hope he gets home soon."

"I pray for him every day. I never prayed before."

"Yeah, war will do that."

"Thank you for your service. It's good to meet one of the heroes."

"I was just doing my part," I tell him. Which is true.

"It was an honor to serve," I say. Which is true.

"How long have you been back?"

"About a year. A little more than a year."

"Are they treating you all right? I worry about that.

On bad nights I worry about Ted not coming home and on good nights I worry about Ted coming home. I read about guys not being treated right. About red tape and having to wait too long and pain," he trails off. Looking at the space that is not my arm.

"I'm doing okay."

He nods, "That's good. I'm glad to hear it."

Cat comes out and as I introduce her I realize I do not know his name. I try not to ask. I have already taken too much. "This is my wife, Cat," I try to leave it there. Leave it alone.

He shakes Cat's hand.

"Andrew," he says.

I stand up and shake his hand again.

"Thank you for stopping. It means a lot," I say. "I'll say a prayer for you. For Ted."

And we walk away.

There are words that should not place themselves in sentences. I made him picture his brother's body. I was complicit. Planting information that is not information. Turning a rumor to a fact. I know that he thinks of me when he shouldn't. That I made my way into his life. Into his brother's life. That I entered something that wasn't mine to enter.

103.

Sometimes it comes out of nowhere:

The sudden heat. Precise. Momentary. I didn't use to notice. That was before I understood how the skies would take her with them. That was before I heard the silence and then the house went up. Now I recognize the change in pressure. The shades of grey.

On Tuesdays and Thursdays I go to the VA hospital. We sit in a circle and everyone says their name. At first I kept trying to explain myself. *It was just a car accident. It happened here.* Which most of them know since I started coming before the accident. One of the guys said, *An arm's an arm.* And they all nodded. And that's that. I still have to say it when someone new comes into the group. One time the guy on my right beat me to it. I said my name and he said, *It was just a car accident. It happened here.* And everyone laughed except for the new guys. They just looked confused.

After the talking most people use the machines. There are special weights. Pulleys and bicycles. A lot of the guys are in chairs or trying to get out of chairs. Nearly everyone has a prosthetic. A newly grown limb they're trying to recognize. To feel. It looks right on them. Even when the stump blisters and bleeds. It's how they get to be whole. To fill their spaces. They take off their arms and push their phantoms into the mirror boxes. An exchange of the lost. A reiteration.

Today the PT is showing me the door knob that fits

onto the steering wheel. She asks if I'm ready. Says that it can be different when it happens in a car. That you can get spooked. That the sooner you get back the better. I tell her I can do it and it makes her happy. It makes her look more relaxed somehow. She tells me she'll order one. She should have it by next week. That she can help me fit it and we can drive around the block. I feel like we've done something big today. That things are getting back to normal.

I feel the scorch as soon as I step outside. That sharp ray of sun. Too sharp for May. Too direct. I look up for the heavy grey. The west sky darkening. Coming for us. The mountains are already gone. I told Cat I'd call when I was done, but I head for the taxi stand. Wait in line.

By the time I'm in a cab the skies are open and I'm soaked through. She'll be gone by the time I get there. It happens too fast here. It's only fifteen minutes home. It will be over by the time I get there. I know she doesn't need me to come home. Still I lean into the proximal. Get as close as I can get.

Hail stones pelt the roof and I see her crouching deeper and deeper. Curling into the smallest place. The driver says he needs to pull over. I tell him he has to keep going even though I can't see out the windshield. He pulls over, stops the meter. I put my head down in my hand. We wait. Him in the cab. Me somewhere between here and home.

104.

A person can only get so small:

After the storm, the waiting. I sit with my back against the door. Telling her I'm here. Telling her I'm sorry I wasn't home when it started but I'm here now and everything will be okay.

"I don't think it's a bad one," I say. "It will be over soon." It's moving away from us already.

When ten minutes pass without thunder or lightning, I tell her, "Now it's only rain." Ten minutes later, "It's over. It's okay now." And I stay, my palm pressed to the floor. I count my breath. Five-hundred. Five-hundred again. She doesn't usually wait so long. She always knows when the storm passes. When it is safe to return. This is the emptiest space. A too large silence. Maybe she cannot exit with me here. Witnessing the door. I move away, "I'll put the kettle on. Come out when you're ready."

Thirty-two steps from her office to the kitchen. Seventeen to get the kettle on the stove. Five to sit. I count fifty breaths. Fifty again. Thirteen steps to turn off the kettle and pour two cups. Thirty-two back to the closet. I put the mugs on her desk and rest my fist against the door. Five breaths. I knock once. "Cat?" Five more. "Cat?" Outside, two birds calling back and forth. The sound of afternoon sun on rainy pavement. "Are you okay?" Only silence and space. "I want you to come out now." Five knocks. "You're scaring me."

I tell myself I'll wait another five-hundred. I breathe it

out. Counting the exhales aloud. "I'm sorry," I say, when I reach the end.

"Cat. Just say one thing. I don't want to open the door. I have to come in now."

My hand on the door knob. Holding it for too long before I turn. "Cat," as the door opens. As I see her insides.

A jumble sale of winter coats. "Cat?" I cannot see her behind the wools and gabardines. I cannot imagine there is room enough for her to stand. Coats press against each other. Each one bulging with pockets and seams. Envelopes and folded paper. Hangers overlapping on three parallel rods. "Are you in here?" Though I cannot see the space where she could be.

I reach in. Elbow and hand forcing a gap between red plaid and pilled blue fleece. Nothing looks familiar. I count seventeen coats on one rack. My hand moves down to the next layer. Twenty-three. Some torn. Some brown around the cuffs. The lowest rack holds twenty-one. Some small. Cracked elastic and chewed-up zipper pulls. Sixty-one. Each one with pockets full of paper.

My fingers stop on an envelope. Yellowed gum. Folded and refolded. The paper inside overexposed. Visible where the flap of envelope folds up in the wrong direction. I can see her handwriting. A *yesterday*. A *promised*. I want to pull the letter free. To calm myself. To find the symmetry of words and sentences. I want to take each piece of paper and divide.

I let the coats fall back into place. Put my hand in my pocket to keep us safe.

105.

The house is full of letters now:

That I would not have opened the door if there was any kind of choice. That I should have waited for an answer. That there shouldn't have been a door to begin with. That there are so many rules around us and we understand the words but not the sentences. That it is okay for there to be a door but there should also be a window. That I am sorry. That I am worried. That I know the ground might give way at any moment. At any question. That I am also made this way. That we may not be the best choices. That here we are.

There is a moment when I think the letters are mine. Before I look at the writing. I do not read the words. Even if I wrote them they are not mine. This is an archive of loss. I do not look at the shapes. How her g's loop back into themselves. How she invents a symbol and sticks with it. How her i's move back and forth as if to make a child stay, as if to grow.

I imagine the names in her hand. *Iago. Ilana. Isaiah. Isam.* All of this without taking a single page from its place. I watch my index finger move across the top of an envelope. *Jackson. Jethro. Joseph. Joshua. Juan.* Testing the edge. Trying to cut. One finger at a time. I don't mean to make the rule but I understand it. It is possible to touch but not to grip. *Kaamil. Kadeem. Kaden. Kadin. Kadmiel.* To know that it is real without removing.

The smell is something like the third floor corridor of

a university library. Dusty and private. If invisible has a smell, this is it. I lean into it. Other people's bodies have occupied these sleeves, these pintucked torsos. I try to find them. Their names. *Lachlan. Lanie. Leena. Logan. Luanne.* Their intentions. *Maha. Mahak. Mahal. Mahdi. Mahsa.* How some of them worry a seam. How some of them carry a pen in their breast pocket. A spilled drink. A decade of cigarettes. I watch my thumb move around a collar. *Nabil. Nabila. Nafisa. Naflah. Naida.* Pull away.

This is her chosen body. She knows me better than either of us thought. One finger at a time, I trace her outlines. *Oliver. Olivia. Omar. Orita. Orrin.* I could draw her from memory. We talk about this. Not a photograph but a map. How only we can make it. How even when the photograph changes, the map might stay just so. How the photograph is science. Light and chemistry. How the map is temporal. Accurate at any moment and also moving. That in the moment when the photograph is developing, perhaps the map, exactly then, somehow meets. How we cannot know or plan to know. How intersections are something worth hoping for. Maybe that's what other people talk about when they talk about faith.

Peter. Petra. Philip. Philippa. Phoenix. She has lived here for a long time. There has always been a door and now I know there have always been bodies. I want to tell her it's okay. That I have also chosen. But how do we speak about it now? I had a body and then I had another body and they were both mine. *Qabil. Qadr. Qamar. Qiana. Qimat.* She is a curator. Collecting forms and contents.

We should have built a house without doors. We should have made the walls from fabric. Here we are. Knowing and not being able to say.

I one-two-three tap down each row of coats. Four-five back up to make it even. Adding up the hangers, making my equations. Dividing them into all the right orders. Making them fit. Making them mine.

Here are some of the rules of being lost: Follow the river downstream. Stay where you are. Cover your head. Try not to panic. If you panic, give yourself ten seconds and then stop. Do not panic a second time. Make a plan. Figure out where you want to be tomorrow. My ring finger has dipped into a pocket. Into an envelope. *Rais. Rakeem. Ramsey. Ranania. Ranit.* Pulling the paper up along the edge. I watch it rise and then I pull away. *Shakil. Shakila. Shakir. Shakira. Shalom.* It is time to leave. I have come too far inside already. I can feel the door against my shoulder and still I'm not sure that I will find it.

I step back and look at the landscape. This lake of coats. This mountain of letters. All of these bodies. This is her refuge. And she's not here. The phone is ringing now. I think it has been ringing for some time. *Thomas. Tobias. Toby. Tom. Tomai.* I close the door.

106.

Some of the things I might have done:

If I had said it straight away. If I had met her at the door. If I had told her about the waiting. If I had right that moment. If I had walked away. If I had not come home. If I had made it home before it started. If I had been in control. If I had waited.

I am in the kitchen and I hear her at the door. My pulse hot in my ears. Beating out the time she doesn't know.

"I'm in here," I call out. A confession.

I hear each step towards. Slow and quiet. She is so small when she walks in. Her tiny sunken shoulders. Her swollen eyes. Almost inaudible, "Hey," not raising her head. Turning back around and out of the room.

I didn't do this. Something else has happened. Something that isn't me.

I follow her to the bedroom. "It was a bad one," I say. "Where were you?"

She shakes her head. Like she can physically shake off the question. "I'm going to lie down."

"I'll bring you some tea," I kiss her forehead. Go back to the kitchen.

I pour out the tea that I'd made before. Put on some fresh water. Wait for the boil. I hope she's sleeping. There isn't room to tell her now. But how to walk around the spaces. How to make her let me in.

When I bring the tea she is curled into the tightest

ball. I put the mug down on the bedside table. Sit beside her. My hand on her hip.

"Are you asleep?"

She opens just a fraction. Turns to look at me.

"I was at my client's house. The one with the mother. It was raining but it just looked like rain, you know. I didn't know it was going to happen. And then I heard the thunder and I said I had to use the bathroom. And then she was knocking on the door and asking if I was okay. I don't know how long I was in there. I couldn't answer. I was sitting in the bathtub. I was so scared she was going to come in. The door was locked but I didn't know if there was a key or some way she could just open the door. I could hear her but I couldn't say anything. I couldn't move. I just sat there with her voice getting louder and louder. I wanted to turn the water on to block her out but I could only think about it. I was stuck."

She looks up at me. The first time our eyes meet.

"I'm sorry, honey. I'm so sorry."

I feel my hands reach behind me. I feel both of them. I feel my right thumb cross over my left.

"When it stopped I thought about climbing out the window. I really thought about it. But I went out there and told her I wasn't feeling well. That I'd fainted. That I'd better go. I could tell from her face she didn't believe me. I was so embarrassed. She asked if I felt okay to drive. I just grabbed my stuff and ran out the door. I sat in my car for I don't know how long. I think she saw me. I just couldn't move. I think she saw me Otis."

107.

This is what it means to be an invader:

To watch the door. To hold a secret. I walk into the house and the first thing I do is check for her. That has always been true. Since we met. I think the first thing she does is check for me too. Maybe it's normal in the larger sense. Needing to know who's in the room. Understanding the territory.

Now when I call out the silence pulls me to the brown door. And if she is home, her voice is like a stop sign. I back away. Not from her but from her knowing.

By the time she got home, with so many eyes on her, so many questions, all I could do was listen. She told me about the houses looking at her. About everyone knowing. Everyone thinking she's crazy. I couldn't tell her about the invasion. I'd been sitting in the kitchen, telling myself to tell her. Reminding myself that I had opened the door because I was worried about her and it's my job to make sure she's okay. But when she told me about the banging on the bathroom door, about the invasion on foreign territory, I couldn't tell her I had also been doing it here. She was looking for ground and I couldn't take this piece away. So I didn't say anything. I made it a secret. There was a moment I could have taken, but I didn't. And after that the truth is harder to come by. It's a danger we all walk.

And now I have a relationship to the room. To the closed door. I won't let myself open it again but I watch it for clues. Run my hand along its hinges. I can only do this if she isn't home. And so if I call into an empty house, I am somehow answered not by her absence but by the door's presence. And I walk towards. Each time knowing I might be found. Each time knowing I might not be able to keep the door closed. That's how it is with secrets. We keep them until we break. And then the scattershot.

108.

She could write, for instance:

About the letters. About the start. About why she keeps them in a closet. About the moment, if there was a moment, when she thought that she might tell me. About how she got the coats into the house. About how she packed them. How she waited for the coast to clear. About times, if there were times, when I nearly interrupted. When I entered a room and she was hiding. About the cover stories and how she kept them from my view.

Maybe there's a letter about the day I left. The day I told her. There would be things in there she hasn't said. Reasons for the form. For finding ways to speak and stay in silence. Maybe there's a letter of return. Something about disappearance. It was always in the air. Even though we both said I'd be safe. Even though we knew it. We were wrong. We haven't talked about it but I know it and maybe she knows it in a letter. Maybe that's her way to say.

There could be a letter from the day we met. The day with all the light. Even though she says she never saw it, maybe she saw it in a letter. Maybe there's a different view. Maybe she doesn't know or can't remember. Maybe she puts them in a pocket and never returns. On to the new words. On to the next.

Maybe she reads them when she's in there. Maybe there's a torch. If I had known, I would have put a light in there. We talked about it when we moved. She said she didn't need it but maybe she was lying. I could have made things easier. I didn't know enough then. And even now, I cannot talk about it. Cannot let her know I've crossed the door.

I don't know where she writes them. I imagine her inside the closet. Sitting on the floor. The torch in her mouth. I don't know where she keeps the blank papers and envelopes. There are so many details. So many questions I cannot ask.

Maybe there's a letter about the numbers. From before we talked and maybe one from after. Maybe that was her way of telling. Of letting me know that she could see and we could make it work. Maybe the letters are for her. Even if there is one with my name. Even if there is one for the numbers. Maybe it's how she works things out. How she understands the landscape. Even so, I want to know. It's not to know the words about me. It's to know the words she makes. It's not the contents of the letters, but the letters themselves. There's never been this space between us. I thought I started it by leaving. But the letters have always been here. And even as I say it, I do not know the always. Maybe this is something new. Maybe the closet was just a closet. It would help to have a timeline. It would help to know the years.

Maybe there are letters for families. Maybe some of this is research. Artifacts and histories. Secret lovers and daughters. Genealogies of want. But every shape is hers. Her imagined hand across a page. Her imagined fingers gripping pencil. Smearing ink. Uncancelled stamps.

Envelopes addressed and never sent. I would know her hand amongst any other. Even as I'm trying to look away. Even as I'm trying to confuse it.

Maybe there are letters about the everyday. About going to a meeting. About research and maps. Maybe there are letters containing the abandoned. All the details that the families do not want to know. All the offerings she makes and puts away. The corridors they do not want to walk. Maybe it's a form of preservation. Keeping everything accounted for and known. Even if there's never any other person. Even if there's not a need. No desire.

Maybe there's something in there that explains the storms. She says she doesn't know but maybe she knows it in a letter. Maybe she doesn't even know it's there. There are too many words to stay inside her. Too many memories and too many pages.

Maybe the closet is to keep them safe. To keep herself from knowing. Maybe she knows it's there and does not want to see. Maybe there's a memory of finding out. Maybe a beginning. There has to be a first storm. Even if she says there isn't. Even if she can't remember. There has to be a moment when it changed. She had to know it then. She didn't have to write it down but if she did she would have kept it in a pocket. Or maybe it came later. The storms and the letters. The coats and the closet.

It's hard to imagine a letter without a storm. I know that geography can be deceiving. That perhaps it's just a matter of making room. Of keeping things where no one else can see them. I have always seen the closet as the place for storms. And so once there are letters the letters are also for storms. Maybe the letters are just letters. Maybe the closet is just a room she knows is safe. Maybe the coats are not as literal as I would have them. Not a shelter. Not a skin to keep her dry. There are so many questions and I will not ask her any. Maybe the letters are an answer. Maybe we can speak inside them. I keep myself from opening her words. From passing through the door and into knowing.

109.

Knowledge can be a choice:

Sometimes you find yourself right on the edge. The place where if you take one more step, you'll be in it. You'll know something new. Most times you don't notice. The movement is too swift. You're just there. Knowing. Or on the road to knowing. But that moment when you could have taken another fork is already past.

I'm trying to make choices. I think about Lanie. About leaning too far in. About interruption. I can't change the road. I can't turn around and I can't stop.

Stopping is what makes her good at her job. Knowing where to dig. Knowing that all the branches matter but that some matter more. She's not about opening doors that don't open. Forcing them. She tries all the doors. She even tries the ones that are hard to find. The invisible portals. But if she gets to a wall, she gets to a wall. She turns around. I envy her that. I know that I should learn from her. And I'm trying.

110.

We make our daily bargains:

Remembering yesterday and other reliable dates. But there's a slippage. A likelihood of reframed memory. This is not an accounting of fault. We are only capable of holding so much. Each new bargain requires an upturned hand. An honest smile. A somewhat cloudy view of everywhere we've been and the sunny trails we've left behind.

We know that the mirror distorts. That the photograph is framed and dependent on machinery. We cannot see ourselves without looking down. We cannot turn ourselves to find the angles. To see what we might appear to be to the person on our left, our right, three steps behind. This isn't about a body. This is about being in a body. About staying. About holding our place.

There's always someone carrying a letter. Someone who has said what they want to say. Mainly to themselves but to someone else if it comes to that. Some people think of it as insurance. Some people think of it as an exit strategy. It never seemed the right fit to me. The words you're willing to say when you can no longer say them. It's not that I don't struggle. Obviously I struggle. But I need a more direct route. A here and now.

There must be a mention of our meeting. The night we got engaged. There must be something about me leaving. About nights when she walked around the house and couldn't feel me. About when I came home.

About accidents and storms. About all of the troubles I do not mean to make. Or maybe they're from a before. Notes from a Cat I do not know.

I don't need to know the contents. I would get stuck in the mechanics anyway. How many lines to a page. How many words to a line. I could see, even without touching, that some of the letters were more than one page. I could guess, even without weighing, that some of them might be the perfect length. Five-hundred unhyphenated words. I know it would unbalance me. That I would fall into them and I would be found.

I know the letters are a problem. I know a person is not meant to have a tiny room full of tiny and less tiny coats. I know the coats are not meant to be stuffed with yellowing and fresh white envelopes. I know that if such a room exists it should not be a room of refuge and it should not be a secret and it should worry the person who finds it and then has to find a way around. All of this is true and so I stay away. Put her in front of me. Between my nervous fingers and the door.

It would have been better to stay. It would have been better if she had walked in the door and found me in the tiny room covered in her tiny secrets. There would have been an explosion and possibly a series of explosions but then there would have been something after that. And I would be there already instead of here. In this unspent space. Toeing the line. Waiting to be helpful. Waiting to be a husband.

111.

It isn't safe to stay inside:

I can tell she's nervous from the tiny bites. She cuts her toast into sixteen pieces. Picks up one piece at a time. Looks at it. Puts it in her mouth. Holds it there for a second before she chews. She doesn't chew a regular amount of times per piece. But it takes her at least a minute to get to the next one. To make herself ready.

"What's going on?" I ask.

"I have to go back there today." She doesn't look up. Her eyes on another tiny piece of toast.

"Where?"

She darts her eyes up. Catches mine for less than a quarter second. Back down to the toast.

"Where I was in the storm. She wants to go over some papers. She wants to do it at the house." She puts the toast in her mouth. Holds. Chews. Swallows.

"Do you think you'll have to be there long?" I don't mean to ask. I don't want to know. I try to cover it. "It looks like a nice day at least."

She looks disappointed. Like I don't get the problem. I do get the problem. But the house is full of letters and she is leaving me alone. I have spent ten days avoiding the door. The only choice is exit.

"I think I'm going to go walking," I say.

And she stops, toast halfway to her mouth.

"I don't think that's a good idea Otis."

"I won't go far. Just to see how it feels."

"Why don't you wait for me to get home. Just for the first one."

"It'll be okay. It'll be part of getting used to things."

She puts the toast back on the plate. There are still eight pieces. She pushes the plate away.

"I'm going to get ready," she says. Stands up and walks to her office. Starts putting things in her bag.

I walk over to her door.

"It'll be okay Cat. It's part of getting better. You'll be okay too."

She nods. Puts her bag on her shoulder.

"Just be careful," she says. And we walk out the door together. Cat to her car and me to the road. To the names.

I walk to the end of the street. Turn left. I keep walking past the next three intersections. I try to think of the M's. *Michael. Michaela. Michelle.* But my mind is in the closet. My mind is poring over coats and letters. I am losing my place. I am trying not to turn around.

112.

I make up a story and make it true:

I get stuck inside the form. Matching the edges. Counting the count. I remember Lanie telling me that other people do it too. They just find a balance. I remember that's what she told me we were looking for. That's why it helped to play the games and to learn how to lose. That I wasn't doing anything wrong. I was just doing one thing too much. I had to make room for something else. And so I learned to lean away from the thing that pulled me. I learned to lean into the places I didn't care about. I don't think it ever changed on the inside. But I found a balance. I found it for a long time.

It's different for every person. I don't expect to find the numbers in Cat's letters or coats. I don't expect to find an order in how many coats in the closet. How many letters per pocket. Per coat. Per rack. I don't expect the numbers to line up. What I mean to say is that I know the letters are her numbers. And the coats. The closet. They're all her numbers. The place that draws her in. That no one else can see and no one has to.

Maybe if I lean into the closet. Maybe the closet is the new balance. Maybe this is marriage. How she pulls me closer to normal without even knowing.

For less than a minute I think it would be good to talk about it. To ask her how it works for her. To ask her if it calms her down. I wonder what she would think about balance. If she would believe it. I play the conversation in my head and I hear her telling me it doesn't work like that. That the numbers are the balance. The letters. The coats. That's what makes our worlds work. That's what makes us possible. I know not to ask out loud. That's the other thing that makes our worlds work. Living without words. Without examining the insides.

I remember a photograph of Cat when she was nine years old. She's on the swings outside her grandmother's house. Wearing a red plastic raincoat with strawberry patches on the pockets. She's squint smiling into the camera. Tom is standing behind her. Her tiny fists balled around the rope of the swing. Her feet pushing out against the air. And I remember the coat in the closet. The strawberries now overstuffed with yellow paper. I remember the writing was that of a child. Slightly oversized and shaky letters. Maybe it's something from her brother. But he was older than the writing. And I imagine his letters as narrow and jagged. A teenage boy's letters. These are something different. Something more innocent. These are the letters of someone who wears a red plastic raincoat with strawberry pockets.

I go through each coat in my mind. I go through each season of our lives. Each photograph of her life before me. I understand the coats as a filing system. But it only works with the coats that belong. There is no reason for the matted fake fur. The series of grey trenches. I make up stories for the coats that were hers and the coats that were mine. I remember coats that belonged to her parents. A coat that was left at a party we had when we first moved into our old place. There was a coat that I think belonged to her cousin. There was one of my dad's. I imagine he must have left it here years ago. I try to remember him asking about it. Me looking around the house. Asking Cat if she'd seen it. I try to remember calling him back and telling him we didn't find it. Maybe he left it in the car. Maybe my mother took it in the house. I imagine Cat being in the room while I'm talking to him. I imagine her walking to the closet. Stepping inside.

I wonder what she does with the contents. The preexistence. Keys and money. Maybe a handkerchief. My dad never went anywhere without a notebook and a pen. Just in case he had an idea for an invention or remembered something he had to pick up from the store. Maybe there's a box for prior contents. Maybe she throws it all away. Do the letters in my dad's coat have something to do with him? Did she think about giving the coat back after he asked? Did she like having him miss it? Did she feel guilty? Is that why there are coats that don't belong to anyone? Did she start collecting them so she could stop collecting what people might miss? Did she feel differently about the coats that were hers? Did they make her feel safer? Did they change the balance?

Every question has a river of answers. Every question has a river of questions. This might be simpler in conversation. If she was answering the questions herself. But it would only be a shortcut.

I don't want to kick her door in. Even gently. Even if she knows I'm right outside.

113.

Stuck in the room and no further:

This time we're both home when it starts. That first rumble. How we look up in unison. As if to see through the ceiling. It isn't raining yet. No flashes of light. No clouded sun. It's somewhere in the distance. Imminent.

We're watching TV and I'm surprised when she doesn't get up straight away. She curls in closer. Another check out the window.

"I think it's still a while away."

"I think so too. I'm okay," she says.

And so we keep watching. Keep listening for the thunder. Ten minutes pass. Maybe more. She jumps at the first brightening of sky. She's out the door without a word. I let her go. I'll join her in a few minutes. But it's better for her to get in there alone. Unwitnessed.

It's already raining by the time I walk into the room. The closet door is open and she's standing in front of it. Breathing hard.

"Cat?"

She doesn't look around. She's staring at the open closet. Her hand on the door. She's shaking her other hand as if to get something off it. Like a spider web. Or drops of water.

"Cat?"

A sound starts somewhere in her throat. A kind of mewling. I walk towards her. Touch her shoulder.

She jumps away from me. Away from the door. Backs towards the window. Eyes wide. Tendons pulling in her neck.

"No No No No No," shaking her head. Her hands pressed against her ears.

I hear the first sharp spike of hail. She can't be out here for this. I don't understand why she's out here.

I walk towards her again, "Cat, you have to go in. It's hailing."

She quickly turns to look outside. A bolt of lightning. As if on cue. She turns back to see me coming towards her. Presses herself back against the glass. Her hands out to stop me from coming any closer. Then her hands up against her throat.

"I can't breathe," she's clawing at her shirt. "I can't breathe."

"Do you want me to go in with you?" I go to take her hand.

She crouches down in a ball. Starts rocking back and forth. Crying. Whispering to herself. I sit down next to her.

"Cat. Tell me how to help you."

She looks up. Meets my eye. Fast and constant inhales. Like she can't get enough or any. Her face streaked with tears. Asking. Accusing.

Is this what it's like inside the closet? Is this what happens in the storms? I would hear this. If this were normal.

She's banging her head on the wall. Eight times on

the wall, then back into a ball, more whispers, back against the wall. I try not to count. Try to stay with her. Not touching but here. Not knowing I know.

114.

She doesn't speak until she has to:

After the lightning. After the thunder. She stays in her little ball. Keening. Rocking. I move over beside her. Reach out and almost put my hand on her back. She curls in and away from me. Moans into her knees.

"I don't know what to do," I say. "I don't know how to help you."

She sits up. Her face swollen. Patched with white and red.

She looks at me. Stands. Walks out of the room. Comes back in with a suitcase. Starts packing up her work.

"What are you doing?"

Her desk is an empty surface. Everything swept inside the case.

She walks out of the room. Comes back with armfuls of clothes. Drops them in the suitcase.

The closet door is still open.

I reach for her arm and she stops me with her eyes.

"Tell me what to do Cat. Tell me what you need."

The closet door is between us. I reach over to close it.

"Don't," she says. "Don't touch it. Don't touch anything."

She looks at me like she's deciding. Walks out again. Comes back with another bag. Picks up the suitcase. And then she's gone.

I hear the sound of rain in the gutters. I hear her car turning over. Wheels on gravel and open doors.

115.

We never said the words out loud but they were there:

I remember asking her about it. Early on. I remember my hand on hers, "We don't have to talk about it now. We can talk about it later. Whenever you want."

She turned around so we were eye to eye. "We won't talk about it later," she said.

I think I blinked, a kind of flinch. She moved closer. Sometimes when I remember this I remember moving back. Just a fraction of an inch. An involuntary movement. But then she was kneeling on top of me and telling me she loved me and pushing my jacket down over my arms.

The rules were clear. We followed them for years without once tripping over each other. I knew it was hers. I knew it was an invasion. Because we did not use words, I made her a promise with actions. And then I broke it.

Every marriage moves through this. An infidelity. A broken trust. Because we don't explain the things we need. Or even when we do. Because we take them on faith. And so by walking through the door I lost something. I am trying to believe we still exist.

116.

I am always moving towards:

Knowing that the closet is somehow connected. That that's where the breaking happened. Either in the entering or the not entering. In the standing outside. The periphery. The precipice.

And now the house is empty and the door is open. And here I am again. With no possibility of interruption.

I feel like she is pushing me towards it. Though she doesn't know. Though she can't. To leave me this alone. To allow this proximity.

It is also the silence. She spent years here without me. She knows how to make her own soundtrack. How to fill the house. The absence of her breath keeps me awake. The absence of her shifting in her sleep.

I am constantly returning. Sometimes physically. To the room but never all the way to the door. Mostly I just see it in my head. Imagine each step closer and closer. Even as I walk. Further from the house. Further from the closet. I try to remember the names but lose track of where I leave off. I reach my hand out to touch a fence. A door knob. I am always there. Running my fingers through pockets. Breathing in the smell of paper and cloth. Maybe I can understand it by osmosis. Maybe I can understand her by where she cannot stay.

117.

I don't know how I got here or how to walk away:

My hand on the door. I am simply here and knowing it. Knowing that one more action is too much. I have moved away from this for three days. The constant pull. The always possible. I have walked myself around neighborhoods. Absented myself from likely access. And here I am. Alone. With hours to spare. Or days.

I return to the closet. I close the door. My hand lingers.

I tell myself I will not read the letters. I will not allow my eyes to focus on any particular word. I will not look at the handwriting. I will not know the recipient or the sender. I will not try to decipher the age of the envelopes. I will not look at postmarks. That much is private. But I know it is more.

I close my eyes as I open the door. The smell of worn fabric. Aged paper. The staleness of air that does not move. I reach out to touch and find gabardine and wool. My eyes are still closed as my fingers find a sharp edge of paper. I open them to red. The thinnest slice through skin. I pull my sleeve down to cover the cut. Thinking it fitting. A justified harm.

I do not want to leave a mark. I should get a band-aid. But I cannot walk away and leave the door exposed again. And I am not ready to close the door. I need to breathe this a little deeper. I need to know why she comes. So I keep my sleeve wrapped around. Careful with everything I touch.

The red plastic raincoat with strawberries on the pockets. Just like I remembered. Just like the photo. An old denim jacket I thought I'd lost. It's harder to stay out of pockets that were once mine. But I do. I move away.

That's when I see the backpack. I don't mean to pick it up. To bring it outside the confines of its room. I put it on the desk. Zippers are still difficult. I hold it down with my elbow and try to open it. It's old. The teeth stiff. It's small enough for a child. Yellow and blue. I have it open now. Papers and papers. I don't know why this disappoints me. I don't know what I was hoping to find. I cannot let myself be this close to words. I pull the zipper closed again. Jagged spurts of movement. And I hear something jingle in the front pocket. Something not paper. The zipper here is already open. The teeth split apart. I reach in and pull out a key chain. A plastic Budweiser bottle opener. An old Toyota key. And something that might be for a house.

C0901120

Dear Otis,

I don't know how to start this. I have started this seven times already and so this is just the one I'm going to send. So that I can. So that it stops.

I know you went into the closet. I know we'll have to talk about it and we'll have to make it okay. But I can't see you now. I can't be in the room with you. When you've been in my room.

I don't want you to write back to me. I'm writing to tell you that I know and that it's something I never thought you'd do. I never thought about putting a lock on the door. It's our house. I'm meant to be able to live there.

We'll figure it out. But I don't know when and I don't want you to push me. I guess I had a panic attack that day. I didn't know what it was. I don't remember very much. But I remember you pushing me made it worse. I'll be ready when I'm ready and then we'll see.

Cat

118.

We have always walked around and never through:

I go to the closet one last time. I don't hesitate. I don't think through the ethics or possible temptations. I just pick up the backpack. This is how it's going to be.

I've driven around the hospital parking lot. Around some back streets. A couple of times with the occupational therapist and once with Cat on the way home. But this is my first time alone in a car since the accident. I don't even realize until I'm outside the house. Turning the ignition. Putting it into gear. My pulse already quick inside my throat.

I think about calling but that would mean pulling over. This isn't about choices anymore. I'm removing the exits. I go to the door. The backpack in my hand.

It takes a few minutes before I knock. I go through the alphabet. One name per letter. I try to think of what to do if she's not there. Or if she won't see me. I come up blank. I do another alphabet and then I'm knocking. And then she's standing at the door. She's not looking at me. She's looking at the bag. All of the color drained from her face. Her lips dry and parted.

"What the hell, Otis? What the hell are you doing?"

I hold out the bag. She takes it. Careful not to touch my hand. She starts to shut the door on me. I step into it.

"Tell me about the bag, Cat."

She keeps pressing the door against my foot.

"Leave me alone, Otis. What the hell are you doing?"
"Tell me about the keys."
She doubles over. Snatches the bag behind her back.

119.

She asks me if I want to read the letters:

I don't. Even when I was in the closet. Even when I was touching the words I did not want to read them. I was careful not to see more than one word at a time. It wasn't the point of it. I wanted to know about the closet. About the coats. I wanted to count everything I could count. Reading the words would have only confused things. They weren't my words. They weren't my way of understanding.

I ask her if she wants me to read the letters. She says she doesn't care. That it wouldn't feel any worse than me being in the closet. She doesn't say it to hurt me but it hurts me. I see her wince when I wince.

I tell her it's better if I don't read them. That she can tell me anything she wants to tell me but I don't want to read the words. I want her to choose the stories. I want her to be in control. She looks tired when I say this. Like I'm shifting the weight of things.

We sit together for a long time. Not talking. I don't want to hear what's in the letters. I want to hear about the letters. It's different. I want to know the shapes but not the insides. I don't feel like I can tell her this. I opened the closet door and it's not fair to close it now. So I sit and wait. It's up to her now. She can pull me further in. It's up to her.

"They're just moments," she says. "I can't remember

all the moments. It would be making things up. There's a letter for every day. So maybe you can just think of a day and that's a day I wrote a letter. It's every day. Every day since I was nine."

Relief moves through me. I don't think we're going inside. I think we're walking the perimeter. Mapping out the general shape.

"I didn't know you when you were nine," I say.

"I was pretty much the same. Maybe sadder."

We're quiet for a long time. It's hard to think of her sadder than this.

"I just wanted to have a brother again. I just wanted to tell him things. One of my teachers said I should try writing him letters. The letters were secrets so I kept them in my pocket. I kept them on me."

Her fingers run over and over the rusted zipper. I'm afraid that she'll cut herself and more afraid to stop her.

She looks down at her hands.

"I thought I was keeping him safe."

I stop myself from speaking. Stop myself from touching her. She threads her pinkie finger through the key ring. Folds her hand over the keys.

"I was afraid that I would keep making bad things happen. After Tom died I knew I was bad. I knew I made things dangerous. But I couldn't tell anyone and I couldn't stop anything. So I kept writing letters and putting them in pockets. The pockets would get full and I'd have to find a new coat. A new hiding place. I'd tell my mom I lost my coat and she'd buy me a new one. I started stealing them from school. I'd save up my pocket money and buy them from the thrift store. I tried to keep myself away from other people. To keep them safe. I kept waiting for my parents to die. I kept waiting for the next fire."

"You're not dangerous," I say. "You've kept me safe."

"I don't know Otis. We're not doing so well. Neither one of us."

C081789T

There were more people than seats. When the man started talking I counted forty-seven people standing up. Your photograph was everywhere. At the front of the room and on little books that everyone held in their hands and put in their pockets. One person dropped their little book on the floor but I picked it up and cleaned it so now I have two.

Everything was pretty. I don't think you would have liked it.

120.

Outside the house and coming in:

I'm trying to remember the door. I remember picking up the backpack. I remember getting in the car. I can't get anywhere between. I don't know what will happen if the door is open or closed. I know she knows I've been inside. The backpack is on her lap. But I don't know what will happen when she sees the closet door.

I turn the engine off. We're sitting in the driveway. Neither one of us moves to get out of the car.

"It was the day of the storm," I start.

She keeps looking straight ahead.

"I got home and I thought you were in there. I sat on the other side of the door and then you didn't come out."

She's still straight ahead. Her fingers on the zipper.

"I sat there for a long time and then I left. I waited in the kitchen."

She shakes her head. Like waking herself up. I think she's going to speak but she doesn't.

"You were in there a long time." I see her head pull back. Like she's trying to line something up. "I mean you weren't in there. I thought you were in there. It was a long time. I thought something was wrong. I knocked. I kept asking if you were okay. I told you I was coming in. I told you."

"It doesn't matter," she says. Still looking ahead.

"I just want you to know."

"So now you know everything," she says. Threading

the backpack onto her left shoulder.

"No."

Silence.

"I just know why I went in the closet. And now you know."

"Okay." And then she opens the car door. And we go home.

121.

She tells me to keep moving so I do:

I stay five steps from her office. Five steps from the door before the door. From questions.

On the fourth morning I am filling the coffee maker and I hear her come in behind me.

"Keep doing what you're doing," she says. "Don't turn around and don't talk."

I put the coffee maker down in my little nest. Place the filter on top.

"Tom and my dad sometimes fought about his drinking. I don't think it was a big thing. I don't think he was a drinker. But he was seventeen so, you know."

I pour the coffee beans into the grinder. Place the lid on top.

"Anyway, Tom came home late and he'd been drinking so they start fighting. I think I was asleep when it started. I remember waking up and there was shouting and the last time that happened Tom was gone for two days."

She stops and I press my hand down on the lid. Grind the beans. Pour them into the filter.

"They were in the living room. I don't know where my mom was. I never heard her."

I check that the nest will hold. Pull it towards me with my left arm.

"I got out of bed to listen. And then I was in his room. His keys were on the bed. I didn't want him to leave so I took them."

I've never done this part in front of her.

"I went back to my room. I could still hear them. My dad telling him it was a school night and Tom saying it was no big deal. It wasn't really anything different."

I get the top of the coffee maker in place. Pull the whole thing closer. Tighter. Start screwing the lid on.

"I put the keys in my backpack. I was going to put them back in the morning. Before school. I just didn't want him going out again that night. I heard his door slam. And my dad still shouting through the door. And then I guess everyone went to sleep."

I take the percolator over to the stove. All without turning around. All without looking.

"We started noticing the smoke around lunchtime. They didn't let us go outside to eat. We had to stay in the classroom. And then parents started turning up at the school. My mom picked me up and we went to her sister's house. They lived in town. Not too far from the school. She said Dad had gone for Tom. That there was a fire in the mountains and we couldn't go home tonight. She told me everything would be okay. That we'd be home tomorrow. That Dad and Tom would be there soon."

I turn the stove on. Walk back to the counter.

"Dad turned up a few hours later but Tom wasn't with him. They sent me to watch TV. I tried to listen but I couldn't hear them talking. At dinner they told me Tom was staying at a friend's place. Everyone's eyes were red from the fire."

I take the rest of the coffee beans back to the fridge. Start cleaning the counter even though it isn't dirty.

"I went to school the next day even though Mom said I didn't have to. There was an assembly and the principal made some of us stand up and everyone clapped like we'd done something. It was still too smoky to go outside so we had to eat lunch in the auditorium. And when I went to put my lunchbox back in my bag I found the keys."

The coffee starts to boil. I walk back over to turn it down. I get the milk out of the fridge. Take her favorite mug out of the cupboard. And one for me.

"I figured I'd put them in his bag or something that night. I wasn't meant to touch his stuff. He was always telling me off for touching things even when I didn't."

I turn the stove off. Keep my back to her.

"But he wasn't there that night either. And the next day they found him on the road. Full of smoke and ash."

She stops talking. I don't know if I'm meant to turn around now. I pour the coffee. Pour the milk.

"They couldn't understand why he was walking. His car was on the street outside our house. We were six or seven miles up the canyon. My mom cried all the time. It was raining hard the night they found him and I remember the sound of her crying and the sound of the rain hitting the window. The flashes of light. They tried to be quiet but she kept asking why he was walking. That he should have been driving. That he would have got out if he'd been driving."

I keep my back to her but take her coffee to the table. Walk back to the stove with mine.

"They only let me see him once. And I wasn't allowed to see him alone. I wanted to tell him I was sorry. I wanted to give him back his keys."

I take a sip of my coffee. Add some more milk.

"That's everything," she says. And I hear her take a sip too.

"That's everything I know."

122.

She writes out the story, writes out the end:

She tells me about the anniversaries. The first few years were all about the rewrite. What if he had not gone out that night. What if they had not fought.

In one letter she waits in his room. He comes in angry. He doesn't want her there. Tells her to get out, to leave him alone. She tells him she had a nightmare. He doesn't want to hear it, doesn't want to share the space. She starts to cry and he sits down on the bed. They play a game of jenga. She goes to bed. He goes to bed. Everyone wakes up and everyone goes to school.

In another version there is no fire. There is a huge storm. There is still a fight but she cannot hear it over the rain and the thunder. The ground soaks through. Everyone is saved. Even the trees.

She writes a letter that starts out just the same as she remembers. All the way through that night. Through the shouting. Through hiding the keys. Through waking up. Going to school. She makes the fire come. Burns the house. Tom is still missing. There are whispered conversations. And then he is back. Riding in a fire truck. He saved a cat. He is a hero now. And everyone is happy.

In one version they are all home when the fire comes. Her parents pack up the car and Tom is looking for his keys. She takes them out of her backpack. Hides them and finds them in a kitchen drawer. They all get out in plenty of time. They spend the night at a hotel watching movies and eating pizza. The house doesn't burn and they all drive home in the morning.

She makes one where he is hurt but doesn't die. She visits him in the hospital and they eat ice cream. She tells him he's the best brother and he tells her she's pretty cool for a kid. He doesn't even have scars from the burns. He is simply well again. Simply home.

She tells me about making a version where her mother finds the keys. Figures out what she did. Why he died. She doesn't write this version down. But she plays it through her future memories. Makes it real but not real enough for letters. In some of the stories they talk about it. In some of the stories her mother knows but doesn't ask. This is her least favorite version. The one she fears the most. The one that may be true without her knowing. She can get stuck inside this one. All of the secret looks. Sometimes her father knows. Sometimes they try to talk about it. To ask without asking. Refusing to know that they know.

In one letter there is no Tom. She leaves the letter unaddressed. She is an only child. She doesn't know what it is to have a brother and she doesn't miss it. There may or may not be a fire but there is no one to get caught inside. No one to hurt. No consequences.

123.

Fingers full of dirt and metal:

We drive up into the canyon. Get as close as memory can get us. We have some tools from the garden but she starts digging with her hands. I kneel down to help but she says she wants to do it herself.

"I barely remember his funeral. I remember the dress I wore. Black velvet with a green satin bow that tied at the back. I only wore it that one time. I always wanted to wear it again but Mom wouldn't let me. She said it was a sad dress. But I thought it was pretty."

The hole is maybe ten inches deep now. She buries her hands in the dirt. Pulls them out again.

"Do you want to say something?" I ask.

She's shaking as she reaches into the bag, pulls out the keys. She unthreads the car key, then the house key. Slips the key ring into her pocket.

"I'm sorry, Tommy," she says. Placing the car key at the bottom of the hole. "Don't be mad," the house key next to it. "I just wanted you to be safe. You always kept me safe," as she moves the dirt back over the keys. Filling the hole. Patting it down.

When we get home she pins the key ring over her desk.

124.

There's room inside the room, letters in the letters: Everything visible. Spilled out of the closet. Out of the pockets.

She is sitting on the floor. There is a stack of six boxes beside her. 1989-1994. She is working on 1995. Pulling letters out of pockets. Smoothing out the paper. Sometimes reading. Sometimes passing over. She makes a pile for each month. Gathers them up in order. Files them in their box.

There are three piles for the coats. Return to Owner. Recycle. Keep. The strawberry coat is the only one in the Keep pile. The pockets empty now. I ask her about Return to Owner. Whether it might not be easier to recycle everything. To start again.

"I want to give things back to people," she says. Not looking up from the papers. "I want to put things back how I found them." She picks up a yellow trench coat. Pulls a stack of envelopes from an inside pocket. "I got this one from the café down the street. Maybe we can go there for lunch and I'll put it back." She puts it in the Return to Owner pile. Picks up a motorcycle jacket.

"We don't have to tell people anything. I'm going to tell your dad we found his when we were cleaning up. And those ones," she points to three ski jackets, "are Aunt Dani's. I'm going to tell her I borrowed them and forgot to give them back." She checks each pocket again. "There's a lot of them though." She points to a tweed sports coat, “That one has to go back on the 206 bus. I’ll do that one tomorrow.”

She pulls a stack of envelopes from an inside pocket. Checks the dates. Stops to read a letter then carefully folds it back into its envelope.

“It’ll be okay. I can do this.”

She looks up at me now.

“You could put those back in the closet for me,” she says, pointing to the early years.

The closet door is open. There are still two racks of coats to go through. But there is room on the left side. She has made a space.

I pick up 1989. My right arm underneath. My left holding it against me. I take it to the closet. And then the next.

Lisa Birman is the author of *For That Return Passage—A Valentine for the United States of America*, co-editor of the anthology *Civil Disobediences: Poetics and Politics in Action*, and has published several chapbooks of poetry, including *deportation poems*. Her work has appeared in *Revolver, Floor Journal, Milk Poetry Magazine, Trickhouse, Poetry Project Newsletter,* and *not enough night*. Lisa served as the Director of the Summer Writing Program at Naropa University's Jack Kerouac School of Disembodied Poetics for twelve years, and continues to teach for the MFA in Creative Writing. *How To Walk Away* is her first novel.

Made in the USA
San Bernardino, CA
07 February 2017